Darcy's Christmas Scheme

By Zoe Burton

Darcy's Christmas Scheme

Zoe Burton

Published by Zoe Burton

© 2021 Zoe Burton

All Rights Reserved. No part of this book may be reproduced in any form, except in the case of brief quotations embodied in critical articles or reviews, without permission from its publisher and author.

Early drafts of this story were written and posted on fan fiction forums in December 2021.

ISBN-13: 978-1-953138-22-4

Acknowledgements

First, I thank Jesus Christ, my Savior and Guide, without whom this story would not have been told. I love you!

Thank you so much to my friends, Rose and Leenie, for their encouragement over the years. I love you both than I can say.

Thank you also to my new friend, Karen, who acted as my accountability partner for this book. Here's to the beginning of an awesome friendship!

And finally, I can't go without thanking my Patreon supporters. You all are an awesome – and patient – bunch!

Chapter 1

Netherfield Park

December 17, 1811

Fitzwilliam Darcy stepped out of his traveling coach and glanced briefly at the handsome house before him. Shivering as a blast of cold swirled around him, he turned, extending his hand into the equipage. When his sister laid her palm in his, he wrapped his fingers around it and assisted her in descending. Then, he repeated his actions, helping Georgiana's companion out, as well.

"It is a very pretty house. Are you certain Mr. Bingley does not mind that I came with you?" Georgiana Darcy turned her big blue eyes up to her elder brother. She bit her lip.

"I am certain. He wrote that he was pleased to host you. I showed you his letter." Darcy grasped his sister's hand and tucked it under his elbow. "All will be well."

With an uncertain nod, Georgiana took a deep breath. "Very well. Shall we go in, then?"

The trio made their way up the set of shallow steps to the door, which opened the moment their feet touched the top step.

The housekeeper stood beside the door and curtseyed. She opened her mouth to speak, but a voice booming from further down the hall stopped her.

"Darcy! How good it is to see you!"

Darcy's face lit with a smile at the sight of his friend. "You, as well." He bowed to the other gentleman. "You remember my sister?"

"I do!" Charles Bingley stepped up and took Georgiana's hand. He bowed over it, rising with a bright-eyed grin. "You have grown since I last saw you."

Georgiana blushed but returned his wide smile with a shy one of her own. "I have, but as it has been a good two years, that is not terribly surprising."

Darcy and his friend laughed. "She has you there," Darcy pointed out.

"That she does, that she does." Bingley clasped his hands behind him and rocked back on his heels for a moment. "We are all in the drawing room with a tea tray and cakes, if you would like some sustenance right away; or, I can have Mrs. Nichols lead you to your rooms, if you would rather warm up and change your clothing first."

As Darcy removed his greatcoat, scarf, gloves, and hat and handed them to the waiting housekeeper before turning to assist his sister with her outerwear, he eyed his friend. "Are you still determined to attend the assembly in the village tonight?"

"I am, indeed." Bingley brought his hands around and rubbed them together. "I am determined you shall meet Miss Bennet as soon as may be. I am certain your doubts will vanish the moment you see us together."

Darcy sighed to himself. He turned to Georgiana and her companion. "Do you and Mrs. Annesley mind staying here alone this evening?"

Both ladies shook their heads, with the younger reassuring her brother. "We will not mind a bit. We will order up warm baths and take our meals on trays, if that is acceptable to Mr. Bingley. Do you not think that a lovely way to spend the end of a long and cold day of travel, Mrs. Annesley?" Georgiana turned to her companion.

"It sounds quite heavenly to me." Mrs. Annesley smiled warmly at her charge.

"It is perfectly acceptable to me! I desire you to treat my home as your own. Anything you wish for, you need only request of my staff and it will be granted." Bingley bowed to the ladies again before looking at Darcy. "Well, old man?"

Shaking his head, Darcy conceded. "As long as my sister is happy to remain at home, I will gladly go to the assembly with you and meet this angel of yours."

"Excellent!" Bingley clapped his hands before gesturing his guests toward the drawing room. "I will give Mrs. Nichols her orders after I allow you to greet my family."

"Lead on, my friend." Darcy offered an arm to his sister, and with Mrs. Annesley following, escorted her down the hall behind Bingley and into the warm room where Miss Bingley and the Hursts were waiting.

Darcy bowed to the assembled family while his sister and her companion curtseyed.

"Oh, Mr. Darcy! How good of you to come for a visit." Caroline Bingley languidly rose from her curtsey with an insincere smile on her face. She gestured toward the sofas and chairs that surrounded the fireplace. "Do be seated."

"Thank you." Inclining his head, Darcy led his sister to the chaise lounge directly beside the fire. He helped her sit, then assisted Mrs. Annesley into the spot next to her charge.

As he did so, he listened with half an ear to the Hursts' greetings. He returned the offered salutations, then seated himself opposite the fireplace from his sister, which happened to be in a chair beside the sofa on which Reginald Hurst was sprawled.

"Chilly day to be making a trip, eh?" Hurst sat up when he noted the tray with fresh tea makings enter the room, followed by trays of sandwiches and cakes.

"It was." Darcy shivered. "I cannot re-call a mid-December when it was so cold. I had the bricks re-warmed when we stopped to change horses, but they only retain heat for so long. I was happy to arrive."

Hurst nodded. "I dislike traveling this time of year, and though Louisa and her sister complain about the size of this house, I far prefer staying here to venturing back to town." He glanced toward his sister-in-law, who was speaking sharply to one of the maids. "I am certain that by the time the season begins, I will have changed my mind."

Darcy nodded, his expression som-ber. Residing in the same house as Caroline Bingley was difficult enough in warm weather, when one had the ability to walk out at will. She had a tongue like a razor and was not shy about using it to slice those around her, no matter who they were. His attention was drawn in her direction again when she began to complain to her brother.

"Really, Charles, to insist we attend another assembly in this insipid little burgh, and on the day your guests arrive, is too much. We would be better served staying at home and allowing Mr. Darcy and his sister to rest." Caroline poured cups of tea as she spoke, handing them to her sister to deliver to those who wished to drink some.

"Darcy has already agreed to attend; you may stop whining. If he does not mind, it cannot matter to you." Bingley raised his brows along with his teacup.

Caroline huffed as she set down the teapot and began placing sandwiches on plates. "Why he would agree to such nonsense is beyond my ability to understand. He is far more cultured than anyone he will meet."

Bingley set his cup into its saucer with an audible click. "He is sitting right here, Sister. He is not an imbecile, and I will not have you treat him so. You may take your superiority and stuff it!"

Everyone in the room became quiet at that point, and all eyes turned to Caroline to see what her reaction would be.

With a sniff and a lift of her nose, Miss Bingley defended herself. "I am aware of Mr. Darcy's position within the room, Charles. I intended to say to him personally exactly what I said to you, when the correct moment arose. As for superiority, we are superior to the residents of this area. There is not a single lady with any degree of accomplishment in the neighborhood. The gentlemen are unfashionable and barbaric. Even Miss Bennet has little to recommend her, apart from her looks."

"Enough, Caroline. I do not wish to hear more and I am certain no one else does, either. Eat your cake, drink your tea, and go change your gown. We are going to the assembly."

By now, the rest of the party was feeling all the discomfort of witnessing such an argument. They ate and drank in silence, and more quickly than they were wont. Within a few minutes, Darcy had risen, taking his sister's and Mrs. Annesley's plates and cups and returning them to the tea tray.

"I will escort Georgiana to her rooms, if you will direct us there, Bingley." Darcy kept his eyes on his friend, making clear to the rest of the room's occupants that he did not wish to spend any more time than necessary with Caroline, who by rights should have been the one to show him to their accommodations.

"Certainly!" Bingley hopped up. "Come with me, if you please." With a sweeping gesture, he herded his friends to the door. He stopped for a moment to whisper to the house-keeper, who was standing sentinel just outside the room, waiting for the summons to collect the trays. When Mrs. Nichols had murmured a reply, he nodded toward the stairs. "You are in the same wing of the house that we are. Come along."

The ladies led the way, with Darcy and Bingley following.

"I am sorry about Caroline." Bingley spoke softly to his friend. "She grows more and more cold with each passing day. I am beyond horrified that she would speak of you in such a manner, especially with you sitting right there." He shook his head. "How may I make amends?"

"Do not worry; she is easily enough ignored. If she is like others in the higher circles, and I know she is, she delights in mocking and scorning everyone around her." Darcy shrugged. "If she is hoping to impress me with her manners so I will offer for her, she is bound for disappointment. I could not tie myself to such a negative person." He stopped, laying a hand on Bingley's arm so that he, too, stopped, but one step up. "I have told you this before, but it bears repeating: no matter what scheme she might concoct, I will never marry your sister."

Bingley nodded. "I know. I have told her this, and that is, perhaps, her reason for behaving so poorly in front of you."

Darcy began to ascend once more. "That may be. It is hard to tell with Caroline."

Within moments, the trio stood in front of Georgiana's set of rooms. She and Darcy thanked Bingley for his care, with Darcy indicating he wished to speak to his sister before retiring to his own rooms across the hall. Bingley reminded him of the time the carriage would leave, then bowed and made his way to the staircase, whis-tling as he went.

"Let us wait in your sitting room for a moment while your maid and the servants get your bath ready." Darcy opened the door and led the ladies inside.

Immediately, Mrs. Annesley curtsied and excused herself to her bedchamber, which was positioned on the opposite side of the shared sitting room from Georgiana's own.

As Darcy settled his sister into a comfortable sofa, he lowered himself beside her.

"Am I in trouble?" Georgiana asked hesitantly, her head tilted to the side as she bit her lip.

Darcy rushed to reassure her. "Not at all. You have done nothing to earn censure. What I wished to speak to you about was Miss Bingley's behavior." He looked his sister directly in the eyes. "She was cruel and thoughtless, and I want to be certain you understand that sort of conduct is never acceptable."

Relief suffused Georgiana's countenance. "I do understand. I dislike that behavior, for I always imagine it is me the person is speaking of, and I would hate to be treated in such an infamous manner."

"Were the girls at school that way?" Darcy's brows creased.

"They were." Georgiana looked at her hands, which were clasped in her lap. "It was touted amongst them as the proper way to behave. The daughters of peers were the worst offenders. I disliked it, but as there was nothing I could do, I tried to ignore them. They did not like me, anyway, because my father did not have a title, and therefore I do not have one. I counted my blessings: at least I had a family that loved me, which was more than many of them could boast."

Darcy's mouth tilted upward on one side. "Indeed, you do have a family that loves you very much. I am happy to hear that you do not participate in that sort of activity. Father would be proud of you."

Georgiana looked into her brother's gaze, with tears gathering in her eyes. "Are you certain? Even after I behaved so abominably this past summer?"

Darcy gathered his sister close. "Even after that, yes. You made a mistake, but you have learned, have you not?"

He leaned back to look into her eyes. "You understand now that pretty words from a gentleman who will not go to your guardian are just that … words?"

Georgiana nodded. "I do understand and I have learned. I will not make the same mistake again."

"Good." Darcy kissed her hair and held her close again before finally letting her go. "I am certain our father would think you the most intelligent young lady of his acquaintance, and he would be spreading your fame to all and sundry."

Georgiana giggled. "Good."

With another kiss for his sister, Darcy left her room for his own.

Chapter 2

Later that evening, Darcy followed the Bingleys and Hursts into the Meryton Assembly Hall. He had never liked such events as public assemblies, but his loyalty to his friend required him to put his own feelings aside, something he gladly did. He thought for a moment of Georgiana, tucked up in her rooms at Netherfield, and smiled to himself. She was doing well. He was grateful for it, which made him even more willing to accompany his friend to a ball.

The gentlemen of the Netherfield party stopped inside the door to the assembly hall, removing coats, hats, gloves, and scarves and handing them over to the young man in charge of the coat room. Louisa and Caroline stepped into the ladies' retiring room to remove their outerwear, giving it over to a young lady to hang up, before removing the pattens off their dancing slippers and checking their appearances in the mirror.

Soon, the group was ready to enter the ballroom, where the sounds of music, laughter, and chatter could be heard coming through the closed door.

They had no more than entered when Bingley began to be hailed from several directions as his neighbors noticed his presence. Soon, Darcy was caught up in a whirlwind of introductions. He did his best to be polite. However, his natural reticence could not be overcome. He simply was not as effusive as his friend. He could only hope he did not cause offense. Though, he thought, why it should matter I do not know. They are not my neighbors.

Caroline and the Hursts did not remain at their brother's side while he made Darcy known to the residents of the area. Instead, they found seats along the wall and settled into them to watch the dancers and, in Hurst's case, to partake of the drinks being carried around by footmen. Darcy was relieved that the trio took themselves off. Caroline's presence had put a damper on things since he'd arrived in Meryton. He could perform much better without her standing behind him.

Before long, Bingley stopped in front of a group of ladies and bowed. Darcy observed the blush that crept over the mien of a willowy blonde and suspected the woman's identity.

"Miss Bennet, it is good to see you this evening." Bingley grinned, his entire focus on the lady before him.

"Thank you. I am delighted that you could make it tonight." Miss Bennet's smile was serene, but her eyes shone as she gazed into Bingley's.

"May I introduce my friend to you all?" Bingley tore his eyes away and smiled at the other ladies in the group.

"You may."

Bingley turned slightly toward Darcy. "Mrs. Bennet, Miss Bennet, Miss Elizabeth, Miss Mary, this is Mr. Fitzwilliam Darcy, of Pemberley in Derbyshire and London. Darcy, this is Mrs. Bennet of Longbourn, and three of her daughters: Jane, Elizabeth, and Mary." Each of the women bobbed a second, quick curtsey when her name was spoken.

As Darcy bowed in response to the curtseys of the ladies, Mrs. Bennet greeted him.

"It is a pleasure to meet one of Mr. Bingley's friends. Welcome, sir."

"Thank you, madam."

"I am sorry my two youngest daughters are not here to greet you. They are already dancing." The matron gestured to the line of dancers in the center of the room. Without waiting for Darcy's acknowledgement, she continued. "Do you enjoy dancing as much as Mr. Bingley does?"

Darcy barely heard Mrs. Bennet's question, for his attention had been arrested by one of the three young ladies that stood with her. He recalled her curtsey at the name "Elizabeth" and assumed that was who she was. He stared, his mouth dry, at one of the most attractive women he had ever met. She was small, the top of her head perhaps reaching his shoulder, with dark hair pinned up in braids and one long curl that dangled in front of her shoulder. She had dark eyes, as well, along with full lips and a rosy complexion. Recalling himself to his location, he heard himself reply, "Dancing? I do not take as much pleasure in it as my friend does." He noted what seemed like relief in the lady's expression. "However," he added, "I could be persuaded to participate, if Miss Elizabeth would join me for a set."

The dark-haired girl blushed a deep red. Her lips compressed for a moment before her features relaxed. "I would be happy to dance with you, Mr. Darcy. Which set did you have in mind?"

"The next, if you are free." Darcy hoped she was. His fingers itched to touch her hand as much as his heart demanded he get to know her.

With a nod, Elizabeth consented. "Very well." She stepped back as though to slip away, but just at that moment, the music faded, indicating the end of the first set.

Darcy tilted his head as he watched her and opened his mouth to ask a question, but Bingley demanded his attention, and so he turned his gaze to his friend.

"Miss Bennet has given me this set. We have a few minutes … perhaps we could walk our partners around the room and then stand beside each other when we dance?"

"What a brilliant idea, Bingley!" Darcy turned and held his elbow out for Elizabeth. "Will you join us?"

Elizabeth looked for a moment as though she wished to turn him down, but after a quick glance at her sister, she nodded and tucked her hand in the crook of his elbow, barely touching his sleeve.

Despite the lightness of her touch, Darcy's heart swelled with feeling to have Elizabeth at his side, holding his arm. He led her behind her sister and Bingley, searching his mind for something to say that would not sound totally inane. He was rarely at a loss for words when he wished to speak and did not know what to make of it now. All he knew was that the woman beside him filled his senses to the point that he could think of nothing but her.

Knowing he ought to say something or be thought a simpleton, he finally blurted out the first thing that came into his head. "There are a number of couples in attendance tonight."

Coolly, Elizabeth replied. "Indeed. I think every one of the four and twenty families in the area are here, as well as many visitors who have come for the upcoming Christmastide holiday. We have not had our little assembly room so crowded in many months."

Darcy nodded but was silent again for a moment. "Do you enjoy dancing, Miss Elizabeth?"

With a tip of her head, the lady acknowledged that she did, indeed, like dancing very much. "It is quite fun to spin and hop around, and I am happy I did not have to give up all of my childish actions when I became an adult." The corner of her lip tilted up.

Darcy chuckled. "I have never thought of the exercise in that manner, but now that you have described it that way, perhaps I should. I certainly enjoyed such activity as a child, myself."

Elizabeth said nothing, but her brow arched in a way that delighted her partner.

Before long, it was time for the dancers to line up, and Darcy deposited

Elizabeth beside her sister, bowed, and stepped across to the gentlemen's side of the floor to stand beside his friend. He smiled when the music began and the dance pattern was called. It was to be a slow dance, with steps that would allow for much conversation. He tapped his fingers against his thigh in time to the music as he waited for his turn. His eyes never left his partner. He knew he should not stare but could not help himself.

Darcy watched as she exchanged a glance with her sister, one that seemed to mean something to the pair of them. Then, Elizabeth turned her head and fixed her gaze upon him. His heart skipped a beat.

"Well, Mr. Darcy, we have spoken of the number of couples and the size of the room. What shall be our next topic of conversation?"

Darcy's lips tipped up. He liked her playful manners. "Shall we speak of books?" He reached for Elizabeth's hands as their turn to move finally arrived.

"Oh, I cannot think of books while dancing. My mind cannot focus on such a thing while my feet are in motion." A smile flashed over her lips for a moment before the steps briefly pulled her away.

Darcy, who had to turn another woman around while a gentleman who was not him spun Elizabeth, felt a sudden arrow of jealousy. He did not like anyone else touching her. The thought brought him up short, and he was quieter when they came back together than he had been.

For a few minutes, his partner seemed content to allow him his silence, but eventually, she took him to task. "Are you well, sir? You have grown quiet. Has someone offended you?"

If only you knew, Darcy thought. Out loud, he replied, "I am well. It is only that something occurred to me that drew my attention away. A feeling, if you will, that I am unfamiliar with. For now, though, I shall put my ponderings aside and give you my complete and undivided attention. Do forgive me for my lapse." He smiled at her, happy to have her hand in his own once more.

Elizabeth eyed him speculatively but said nothing else on the matter.

"If you do not wish to speak of books while dancing, what topics are available for us to canvass?" Darcy glanced at his partner out of the corner of his eye as they promenaded down the line behind Bingley and Jane. "Shall we speak of your family? Will you tell me of your sisters?"

Elizabeth shrugged. "Certainly. Jane, as you know, is dancing with Mr. Bingley. She is the eldest of us and is very kind. She sees only the good in others, and I fear she may be hurt one day as a result."

"By my friend?" Darcy's attention was divided between the woman at his side, Bingley and Miss Bennet ahead of him, and keeping his feet moving appropriately and in time to the music.

Elizabeth was quiet for a moment but eventually admitted her fear. "Yes. It is clear he likes her every bit as much as she likes him, but it is equally apparent that his sisters do not like our family." She shrugged again. "He would not be the first gentleman to live at Netherfield who broke someone's heart."

Darcy bit his lip as he thought. When they turned and began to move back down the line, he tentatively began. "If it is any consolation, I have known Bingley for a long time. He is as honorable a gentleman as any. His roots are in trade, yes, but his father taught him all the best qualities of a good man, and his schooling finished it. We went to Eton and then Cambridge together, though Bingley is a bit younger than I. I would trust him with my sister, if it were me."

Elizabeth's brow had creased as she listened. She took a deep breath.

"Thank you for reassuring me, and allow me to apologize for leading the conversation down this path. It was wrong of me to do so."

Darcy squeezed her hand. "There is no need for an apology. You are a good sister to look out for Miss Bennet so."

"Thank you." Elizabeth's lips tilted up in a brief grin.

Darcy said nothing else, instead basking in the glow of her smile for a time. By now, the first dance was ending. He deposited his partner on her side of the line and resumed his place across from her. His attention was drawn by his friend, who leaned over and quietly spoke to him.

"It seems as though you are enjoying yourself."

"I am." Darcy tore his eyes from Elizabeth to look at Bingley. "Your Miss Bennet seems to like you very much."

Bingley's grin lit up his countenance. "Do you think so? I felt it to be true, but my sisters, Caroline especially, did not agree. Caro dislikes Mrs. Bennet and the younger girls."

"Your sisters would be critical of anyone to whom you took a fancy, unless she had an independent fortune."

Bingley rolled his eyes. "True. I will continue to ignore them, since you have given me encouragement." He glanced across the way to the ladies. "She is an angel. I cannot imagine my life without her in it." He looked at his feet for a second and then back up at his friend. "I do not plan to wait long to propose."

Darcy smiled. "I did not think you would. As long as you love her and she returns your feelings, that is all that matters. You are not marrying Mrs. Bennet or her other daughters. If she ends up being as bad as your sister fears, you can always purchase an estate elsewhere. There is no need to buy Netherfield unless you truly wish to."

The musicians struck up once more, so their conversation came to a halt. The pattern called for this dance was a little bit faster than the previous one, but still allowed for a decent conversation.

"Do I understand correctly that you are the second daughter?" Darcy had much more success getting Elizabeth to speak of her sisters than her own likes or dislikes, so he decided to continue in that vein.

"I am. Mary is next, and the two you did not meet are the youngest."

"Tell me about Miss Mary. Is she as charming as you?" Darcy saw something flicker in his partner's eyes, but it was gone before he could discern its meaning.

"She can be, yes. She does not have a sister she is a bosom friend with, as I am with Jane and Kitty is with Lydia, so she has found her own amusements. She enjoys reading Fordyce and preaching at us all, but I think that is her way of distinguishing herself."

"I see." Darcy thought a moment. "I have a cousin on the Darcy side of the family who is similar. She makes her siblings cringe sometimes, but is a very sweet girl underneath her façade."

Elizabeth nodded, taking his hand and allowing him to lift their clasped fingers above their heads as they turned in a circle. "Yes, that is Mary, as well."

Another moment of silence passed as they completed the next step to the pattern. Then, Darcy asked about the youngest girls. "Your other sisters, what are their names?"

Elizabeth smiled as she glanced around. "Kitty is next to Mary. She is the girl in pink at the end of the line." She tipped her head to the right. "She is a follower, I fear. Lydia is beside her in the light blue. As the youngest, she is quite spoiled by us all. She is the leader Kitty follows." She sighed. "I worry about them, too. Mary will be fine, I think. She will find a young man one day who will not mind a sober and solid wife, but Kitty and Lydia are not deep thinkers." She frowned, falling silent as she looked down the line at the younger girls. "Hopefully, they gain some maturity soon."

Darcy said nothing, uncertain what he ought to say. After a moment, he noticed Elizabeth start, blush, and speak again.

"Do you have any sisters, Mr. Darcy?"

"I do." He tilted his head to look at her. "I beseech you again to not be distressed over your recent speech. It speaks well of your character that you are concerned about all your sisters."

Elizabeth looked at her feet. Just then, their turn to move came up once more and she reached her hands out to him. "Thank you." She smiled and said nothing else.

Chapter 3

After a moment, Darcy shook himself out of the daze he had briefly sunk into when she had looked at him as she had. He cleared his throat, blushed, and cast around in his mind for the topic of conversation. "My sister. Oh, yes." He cleared his throat again. "I have one. Her name is Georgiana and I have guardianship of her, along with my cousin. She is twelve years my junior. She is not out, so she did not come with us. She remained at Netherfield with her companion tonight. I hope to introduce her to you at some point in the future."

"How old is she?" Elizabeth smiled at the gentleman beside him as she curtseyed to him, causing another pang of jealousy to pierce Darcy's heart, a feeling he strove to ignore.

"She is fifteen." He hesitated, uncertain how much to reveal to a woman he had just met, despite how she made his heart pound. "She recently suffered a heartbreak but is recovering quite nicely." He noted a look of sympathy pass over his partner's face.

"She is quite young for that." A burst of laughter from further down the line of dancers drew Elizabeth's attention. The corners of her lips turned down for a moment as she murmured, "Perhaps that is just what Lydia and Kitty need." She shook her head, then, and gave Darcy her attention.

"Yes, she is full young for such an occurrence, but her new companion assures me that time will heal all, so I am confident Georgiana will be well. She was shy and reserved to begin with. It was unnerving the first few weeks when she stopped speaking at all."

A look of sympathy flashed over Elizabeth's face, chased by what appeared to Darcy to be embarrassment and then shame. His brow creased. He opened his mouth to ask her about it when she spoke.

"I am sorry, for your pain, as well as hers." She lifted the corners of her lips for a quick second.

The musicians chose that moment to let the music fade away, ending the set of dances. Darcy flashed a smile at Elizabeth as he bowed to her. Then, he offered her his elbow. She placed her hand in the crook. He led her from the dance floor and toward the chairs in which her mother and some of the other ladies were seated. Once there, he reluctantly let her go, assisting her into a seat and bowing.

Elizabeth smiled up at him. "Thank you for the dances, Mr. Darcy."

"It was my pleasure. May I call on you tomorrow?" Darcy no more than got the words out than his attention and Elizabeth's was caught by Mrs. Bennet.

"Did you enjoy your dance, Mr. Darcy? My Lizzy is an excellent dancer, do you not agree? She is not as handsome as Jane, but she acquits herself very well on the dance floor."

Darcy pressed his lips together. He risked a glance at Elizabeth, noting the look of horror that passed over her features and the rush of redness that rose up her neck and cheeks.

This must be why Bingley's sister dislikes the family, he thought. She should not have spoken so of her child, especially not in public like this. Out loud, he replied, "I did enjoy it. Miss Elizabeth is quite accomplished; we never missed a step. She is an excellent conversationalist, as well. You should be proud of her."

Mrs. Bennet's eyes widened. "Oh." They darted toward Elizabeth and then back. A weak smile lifted the corners of her lips. "Oh, but of course. I am very proud of her. She has many excellent qualities. She will make someone a magnificent wife. Why, I taught her myself how to run a household and plan a dinner party."

Bingley broke in and changed the subject, apparently eager to prevent any discord. Darcy allowed it, knowing as he did his friend's dislike of arguments and bickering. As the musicians struck up another song, both gentlemen bowed to their partners. Darcy approached his friend's sisters, securing a set with each. It was not until he led the eldest of them to the dance floor that he realized that Elizabeth had not replied to his question.

~~~***~~~

In the end, it did not matter that Darcy had received no reply. Though his initial thought had been to remain at Netherfield the following day, the pull he felt to see Elizabeth again was difficult to deny. When Bingley invited him to ride along to visit Longbourn, he jumped at the opportunity. Thus it was that he found himself in the well-appointed drawing room of the Bennet household.
~~~

After greeting the ladies, Darcy and his friend chose seats as advantageous to each as possible. Bingley, of course, gravitated to Jane's side. Darcy was not so content in his choice. Elizabeth was on a settee set back from the fireplace a bit, but Miss Mary had joined her there. His first choice being unavailable, Darcy quickly changed tactics, striding to an empty chair to Elizabeth's right. Settling in after bowing to Elizabeth and her sister, he was pleased to note that though he now had the arm of the piece between himself and the object of his attraction, he was actually closer to her than he would have been on the settee. He smiled to himself.

"Good morning, Miss Elizabeth, Miss Mary. I trust you are well?"

Elizabeth smiled. "I am very well." She turned to her sister. "How about you?"

Mary lifted her chin slightly. "I am, as well. Thank you for asking."

"Excellent." Darcy relaxed a bit now that the niceties were out of the way.

"You did not bring your sister?" Elizabeth tilted her head as she asked.

Darcy shook his head. "No, not today. Not this morning, anyway. She is a late riser and Bingley and I did not wish to wait. I left her a note, explaining where I was and that I would like to introduce you all at some point during our visit."

"How long are you staying?" Mary glanced at Elizabeth as she spoke.

Darcy's eyes followed Mary's, though he had been struggling to stop staring since he entered the room. He forced his gaze back to the younger girl. "We promised to stay through Boxing Day, at least. We may decide to remain throughout the festive season." He allowed his eyes to once again settle on Elizabeth. "Depending on how things work out." He noted Elizabeth beginning to blush.

"I see." Mary glanced at her sister and fell silent.

Elizabeth took up the conversation. "How do you find Netherfield?"

"It is a very fine house. The beds are very comfortable and the rooms are not so large that a good fire cannot heat them."

Elizabeth nodded. "I believe the builder made it as airtight as he could.

I remember my father speaking of it to Sir William after the last tenant left it."

Darcy nodded. "It is a modern build-ing and they are generally good about that. My home in Derbyshire is drafty. Beautiful, but you can feel the air coming in around the windows in some rooms, as old buildings are wont to do."

Mary had been following their conver-sation silently, until now. "Longbourn has a couple rooms like that in the older section. I would imagine keep-ing a large, old house would take quite a bit of time and resources."

"It does." Darcy shook his head but lift-ed his lips at the corner. "It is a con-stant battle. I am grateful to have a steward to oversee it all."

Bingley caught the attention of the trio. "The sun has come out and the drive seems to be drying nicely. Perhaps, Miss Bennet will join me for a walk. Darcy, would you be willing to attend us?"

"Gladly." Darcy turned to the lady sitting beside him. "If I can prevail upon Miss Elizabeth to join me."

Elizabeth's eyes widened. She looked in her sister's direction, and at an almost imperceptible nod from Jane, acquiesced. "I will." She rose with her sister and the gentlemen. "Mary, would you like to come along?"

Mary's nose wrinkled. "In all that dirt? No, I am sorry. I will be here when you get back, though."

Darcy could not see Elizabeth's features, but her voice sounded strained.

He tilted his head, a crease between his brows, and watched her as she turned toward her youngest sisters.

"Do not bother to ask!" Lydia cried. "I agree with Mary. Besides, I suspect too many observers will be unwelcome for this walk." She began to giggle, bending her head close to Kitty's and whispering.

Elizabeth huffed. She said nothing else, however, and within a few minutes, the two couples were dressed in their outerwear and wandering up the lane. She had taken Darcy's arm when he offered it, but once they were down the steps, she let it go. He wished she had not. He enjoyed the feel of it on his arm and longed to touch her again.

They said nothing as they followed Bingley and Jane for several minutes. When it appeared that his partner was trying to catch up to the other couple, Darcy touched her arm to stop her. "Forgive me. Bingley requested this morning that we hang back a little. He would like a private audience with your sister but without the theatrics such a request might cause in the house."

Elizabeth stopped as soon as Darcy touched her arm. Her eyes grew wider as she listened to his speech. Her mouth made an O while her head turned to watch her sister's progress with her beau. She swallowed. "I see." She turned to Darcy. "What shall we speak about then, while we wait?"

Darcy smiled. "Whatever you wish." He glanced down the lane in time to see Bingley turn Jane towards him and drop to one knee. "How do you feel about my friend marrying your sister?"

Elizabeth also peeked at the other couple, and a slow smile began to lift her lips. "I am delighted for her. I hope she will be very happy, though one cannot predict the future." She paused. "They do make a good couple, do you not think?"

Darcy nodded, his own lips rising as his companion's did. "I do. They seem to be very much in love."

"They do." Elizabeth snuck another peek and then turned her gaze toward Darcy. "It was almost instant, I would say, on both their parts. The feelings have appeared to become deeper on both sides as the last weeks have progressed."

"Do you long for such feelings to come to you, as well?"

Before Elizabeth could reply, Bingley and Jane rushed toward them.

"You must congratulate us," Bingley declared. "Miss Bennet has agreed to make me the happiest of men." He lifted Jane's gloved hand to his lips, bestowing a tender kiss on the back.

Elizabeth squealed and reached out to hug Jane. With fond smiles at the sisters, Darcy and Bingley shook hands.

"Congratulations, old man. I would say you have done very well for yourself." Darcy clapped his hand on his friend's shoulder.

"Thank you. Your support means everything to me." Bingley grinned. When Jane and Elizabeth parted, he took his betrothed's hand in his once more. "I must speak to Mr. Bennet immediately."

"Yes, and I must tell Mama. She will be overjoyed." Jane's countenance glowed with her happiness.

"We will follow you." Elizabeth chuckled. "Go now, before one of you bursts a button or something."

Darcy laughed at both Elizabeth's words and Bingley's and Jane's besotted looks. He waved his friend toward the house and extended his arm for his companion to take. He strolled beside her in contented silence.

Chapter 4

The distance to the house from the spot in the garden where they had stopped was not far, and soon they were entering the doorway. Darcy noticed Bingley ducking into Mr. Bennet's book room as he handed his coat to a maid. He helped Elizabeth out of her pelisse, handing that over, as well, then followed her into the drawing room in time to hear Jane tease her mother.

"I do not know where Mr. Bingley went." Jane's smile was, as always, serene. Only the crinkles around her eyes gave her feelings away.

"How can you not know?" Mrs. Bennet's hands landed on her hips. She looked around and, seeing Darcy escorting Elizabeth into the room, appealed to her second daughter. "Lizzy, what is happening? Mr. Darcy returned with you, but Mr. Bingley has disappeared. Did he propose?"

"I do not know, Mama. We became separated and I could not hear their discussion." Elizabeth spoke calmly as she seated herself and adjusted her skirts. She glanced up at Darcy when he sat down beside her, giving him a small smile.

"You left Mr. Bingley and Jane alone?" Mary's horrified question drew the attention of everyone in the room.

Darcy saw Elizabeth roll her eyes, though she replied gently enough.

"I did not say that. I could see them perfectly, but I was too far behind to hear their conversation." She shrugged. "Besides, they spoke quietly between themselves. We do not all shout, you know."

"Oh, never mind that!" Mrs. Bennet bustled over to Elizabeth, stopping a few feet away. "What did he do? Did they just talk?"

Lydia called out a question from the other side of the room. "Did he get down on one knee?" She turned to Kitty and covered a giggle with her hand.

Mrs. Bennet whirled around from looking at Lydia to stare again at Elizabeth. "Well, did he?"

Elizabeth's shoulders lifted. "I do not know. You will have to ask him."

Mrs. Bennet threw her hands into the air. "Oh, how you delight in vexing me! You are so much like your father that I do not know what to do with you." She huffed and marched to the seat she had been occupying when the four young people had originally walked out. "I suppose we shall have to wait for him to return."

The matron had no more than plopped herself down into her chair when the door opened, and Mr. Bennet entered, followed by Mr. Bingley. Darcy and the ladies rose to their feet.

"Well, Mrs. Bennet. You are about to be made very happy. I am pleased to announce that Mr. Bingley has requested the hand of your daughter in marriage, and Jane has accepted him." The patriarch extended his hand to his eldest and, when she placed hers within, drew her to stand between him and her newly betrothed.

"They have expressed a desire to marry in late January."

Mrs. Bennet had stood, silent, as her husband was speaking. Darcy was shocked that she managed such a thing, but could clearly see how hard she worked to repress her reactions. Until, that is, Mr. Bennet stopped speaking. Then, her effusive response was strong enough to make Darcy step back, happy he was not the recipient of such attentions. He stood apart for a few minutes as first the matron and then her daughters congratulated his friend. He did not notice the elder gentleman slip away from the group until he had approached.

"My wife's reactions tend to be rather … enthusiastic. Do you not agree?"

Bennet's lips twisted into a sardonic smirk.

"Indeed, they are." Darcy winced as a particularly loud squeal pierced his eardrums.

Bennet chuckled. "One becomes used to it after more than two decades. She has improved over time; she used to interrupt me before I could finish."

Darcy's brows rose as he looked from the group near the door to his host. "She acquitted herself admirably today, then. I could see she was holding herself in check."

Bennet laughed again. "She did. I confess I take delight in dragging things out most of the time. I took pity on her today." He nodded toward Jane and Bingley, still being hugged and congratulated as his wife chattered without ceasing. "She has hoped for one of our girls to marry for a long time. She has already experienced two disappointments. I could not draw it out too long and cause another."

Darcy's brows rose as he half-nodded in acknowledgement of the elder gentleman's words. "Indeed. Allow me, then, to congratulate you and your wife for a successful attachment."

"Thank you, though I require no such felicitations." Bennet chuckled. He tipped his head toward the newly formed couple and winked. "Now that I have made my wife happy, I intend to slip off to my book room." He bowed. "Until next time."

Darcy returned Bennet's bow and murmured a reply. He watched the other man tiptoe away and then looked toward his friend. Seeing – and hearing – that Mrs. Bennet's effusions had waned, he took the opportunity to approach Bingley and Jane to congratulate them once more.

"Congratulations again, Bingley. And to you, Miss Bennet. I wish you both very happy."

Bingley and Jane beamed at him. "Thank you," Bingley replied, his arm snaking around his betrothed's back for a quick second. "I know we will be." He briefly gazed into Jane's eyes, adoration written all over his countenance.

Darcy watched for a long moment, amused at how quickly they became lost in each other, before he finally chuckled. "I think I will go back to Netherfield and see my sister, once I have taken leave of our hosts." He laughed out loud when his words snapped the couple out of their stare.

"I apologize, sir." Jane spoke softly, a blush causing her face to redden. "Thank you for your felicitations."

"You deserve them. Bingley is a fine man, and I know he will do his utmost to make you happy." With another smile and a bow, Darcy took his leave of the couple. He walked a few steps away, eyes darting around the room, looking for Elizabeth. Noting her location, he made his way to her side.

"I must take my leave of you, Miss Elizabeth. I thank you for your company and your conversation today." Darcy bowed.

Elizabeth set down the embroidery she had taken up after hugging her sister and looked at Darcy. She lifted her lips in a small smile. "I was glad to render a service to your friend and my sister."

Darcy returned her smile. He wished to say more, but was prevented by Mrs. Bennet.

"You are not leaving, Mr. Darcy? I have invited Mr. Bingley to dine with us in celebration. You must join us!"

"I am sorry, madam, but my sister needs me today to help her settle in at Netherfield. I thought to come back tomorrow, though, and bring her with me, if that is acceptable?"

Mrs. Bennet clapped her hands. "You have a sister? How wonderful! She is more than welcome to visit at any time." She paused. "As a matter of fact, I invite you both to dine tomorrow. I will send notes around to our closest friends and we will have a dinner party. Yes, that is just the thing!" Nodding happily to herself, the matron settled back into her chair.

"Thank you." Darcy bowed. "I accept for both of us. Until tomorrow, then."

Darcy looked around once more to see that Elizabeth had been watching his interaction with her mother. He could not decipher her feelings from her look, but he drank in her fine eyes for a moment before bowing again and exiting the room.

~~~***~~~
~~~

Upon his arrival at Netherfield, Darcy immediately sought out his sister. He found her in the drawing room with Mrs. Annesley, Miss Bingley, Mrs. Hurst, and Mr. Hurst. He bowed and greeted everyone. As he spoke, he carefully examined Georgiana's mien and thought he detected a bit of strain around her eyes and mouth.

"Good afternoon, Mr. Darcy. How good of you to grace us with your presence." Caroline's normally languid tones sounded more like sarcasm today. "I was just telling dear Georgiana about my coming out. There is nothing like preparation to make one's own event a success, and since she has no mother, I thought it only fitting to assist her in her education."

Darcy grew stiff as he listened. "Georgiana will not be making her come out for two or three years. There is plenty of time for her to learn what to expect. I thank you, though, for your efforts." He strode to his sister's side and proceeded to take up the place next to her.

Miss Bingley sniffed. "You have proven my point, sir. As a male, you have no idea what is involved for a member of the opposite sex. Your sister requires female guidance." She glanced at Mrs. Annesley, flicking her eyes up and down the companion's form. "From someone with experience and who understands the requirements."

Darcy gritted his teeth. He paused before he spoke, hoping to control the vitriol that danced on his tongue. "I will take your opinion under advisement. Thank you." He turned the conversation away from Georgiana. "Your brother wished for me to tell you he will be dining at Longbourn tonight."

Caroline tsked. "At Longbourn again?" She shook her head. "I wish he would not go there so much. It can lead to no good."

Darcy said nothing to this, instead requesting a moment of his sister's time. "I have something I would like to discuss with you. Will you join me in the library?"

Georgiana swiftly agreed, and Darcy stood to assist her in rising. He turned to Bingley's sisters. "We will leave you for now. Mrs. Annesley, my sister will not require your services for at least an hour. You may have this time for yourself." He watched as the companion nodded before rising, curtsey-ing, and leaving the room.

"We dine at eight." Caroline had re-sumed her air of ennui, and her voice was back to its usual languid tones.

Darcy merely nodded and bowed be-fore escorting his sister out of the room and across the hall. He closed and locked the door behind them.

Georgiana headed straight for the seating area beside the fireplace, set-tling into the corner of a sofa. "Thank you for rescuing me." She patted the seat beside her.

Darcy smiled as he immediately took his place at his sister's side. He reached for her hand, cradling it gen-tly in his. "Miss Bingley was unkind?"

Georgiana shook her head. "Not un-kind; overwhelming. The moment I entered the room, she began to be-have as though I were her child. Her unschooled child, at that. Mrs. Annes-ley tried a few times to redirect the conversation, but ..."

"Miss Bingley was unstoppable." When Georgiana rolled her eyes and affirmed his supposition, Darcy squeezed her hand. "I apologize for not returning sooner. I could have saved you an afternoon of pain had I done so."

"All is well, Brother." Georgiana laid her free hand on Darcy's, after ma-neuvering herself to face him, one knee resting on the sofa. "You are here now, and I know you do not in-tend to leave me at the mercy of our hostess unless you have to."

"I do not." Darcy tilted his head. "We have been invited to Longbourn to dine tomorrow. I have accepted on your behalf. I hope that is pleasing to you?"

"Of course." She raised her brows. "Longbourn is the home of the lady Mr. Bingley likes?"

"It is." Darcy hesitated. "I should probably not tell you this, and make sure you do not share it with anyone, not even Mrs. Annesley. Promise me?"

Georgiana's eyes sparkled at the thought of a secret. "I promise! What is it?"

"Bingley proposed to Miss Bennet today, and she accepted him."

"He did?" Georgiana sat straight up and clapped her hands. "How exciting! Is that why we are going to dine there tomorrow?"

"It is." Darcy grinned at his sister's excitement. "Mrs. Bennet invited me for this evening, but I felt a need to spend the time with you. She was happy to have us tomorrow. In fact, she plans to invite some of the neighbors and make it a celebration."

"Oh." Georgiana bit her lip.

Immediately sensing the problem, Darcy reassured her. "Do not fear. It is a bit formal for a young lady who is not out, but Miss Bennet's sisters will be there, as well, and the youngest is not much older than you, if at all. Though you are not out, this is a special occasion. I will be there, as well, and I promise to protect you from unwanted attention, as much as I can.

You may look to me if you are uncertain about anything."

Georgiana nodded. "Thank you. What are Miss Bennet's sisters like?"

Darcy paused as he considered what to say and how to say it. "There are five Bennet sisters. Miss Bennet is the eldest, of course. Next is Miss Elizabeth. She is …" Darcy thought a moment. "She is fascinating. Just as beautiful as her elder sister, and very witty."

Georgiana tilted her head as she watched the expressions crossing her brother's face. "That is high praise. You must like her."

Darcy blushed. "I do, as a matter of fact. I felt an instant connection." He shook his head. "I have never felt such a thing before. I hope to get to know her much better and see what sort of character she has."

Georgiana smiled but said nothing else about Elizabeth. "What about the rest of the sisters?"

"Well, Miss Mary is next, I think. She plays the pianoforte, but without much feeling. Her playing is ponderous. She is quiet, or has been so far, at least in my presence. She has be-haved with propriety. I know nothing else."

Georgiana dipped her chin. "Who is next?"

"I am uncertain who is youngest, but the last two are Miss Kitty and Miss Lydia. Miss Lydia is the loudest." He hesitated. "She is rather immature, in my opinion, but she is very much like her mother, who I will tell you about in a moment. Miss Kitty is quieter but still involves herself in Miss Lydia's folly."

"Hmmm," Georgiana murmured. "I knew girls at school who were immature. Does Miss Lydia giggle at everything?"

"She does. She is often loud and a bit brash, as well. Bold would be a good word to describe her."

"How is she like Mrs. Bennet?"

Darcy rolled his eyes. "Mrs. Bennet is loud and more than a bit brash. If I had met them before Bingley formed an attachment to her daughter, I would have advised him to leave the area forthwith. I can see, though, that she loves her family. If she has be-haved in a mercenary manner, I see no evidence of it." He sighed and brought his focus back to his sister. "Anyway, be warned that Mrs. Bennet might feel every bit as overwhelming at first as Miss Bingley."

Georgiana nodded, a small smile playing over her lips. "I will." She paused and watched her brother for a moment. "Are you certain we cannot visit today? I should like very much to meet Miss Elizabeth, since she has captured your attention so thoroughly."

Darcy drew his brows down in a mock frown. "I never said she captured my attention thoroughly."

Georgiana giggled. "You did not have to. I could see it written all over you."

Darcy wiped his hand from his forehead to his chin, making a funny face at her as he did so. He grinned at the peal of laughter that escaped her. "It is good to see you in such fine spirits." He grasped her hand again. "You are feeling better."

Georgiana squeezed Darcy's fingers. "I am, both physically and emotionally. Thank you for your care and patience." She leaned over and kissed his cheek. "I love you."

Darcy returned his sister's gestures. "I love you, as well." He rose from his seat. "Shall we go upstairs to change for dinner?"

Georgiana glanced up at the clock on the mantel. "I suppose we should." She accepted Darcy's hand and he helped her to rise. The pair ascended the staircase together.

Chapter 5

The next day, Darcy and Georgiana arrived at Longbourn with Bingley. Darcy had protested that it was too early in the morning for near-strangers to call, but his friend insisted the family would not mind. So, he and his sister boarded the carriage with Bingley, arriving at the neighboring estate in time to eat with the Bennets as they broke their fasts. Immediately upon entering the house, Darcy sought out Elizabeth.

"Good morning, Miss Elizabeth." He bowed low, his happiness great at seeing her fine eyes so early in the day.

Elizabeth's lips lifted at the corners in a small smile. "Good morning." She glanced at Georgiana, smiling at her, then returned her attention to Darcy.

"Will you introduce me to your companion?"

"I will!" Darcy grasped Georgiana's elbow and pulled her a bit closer. "This is my sister, Miss Georgiana Darcy." He turned to his sister. "Georgiana, this is Miss Elizabeth Bennet of Longbourn."

Elizabeth curtseyed to the young girl. "I am pleased to meet you."

Georgiana returned the greeting. "I, as well." She lowered her eyes.

Elizabeth tilted her head, gazing at the younger girl for a moment, then gesturing to the sideboard. "Are you hungry? We have plenty, and I heard Mama asking for more from Mrs. Hill." She paused, waiting for Georgiana to look up. "Would you like to sit beside me? Perhaps your brother will sit on your other side, if we ask him to."

Darcy promptly agreed. "Of course, I will."

A slow but tentative smile lifted Georgiana's lips. "I would love to sit between the pair of you."

"Excellent!" Elizabeth hooked her arm through the other girl's and they made their way to the table.

Darcy followed, pleased to see his beloved sister being taken under the wing of the woman who was worming her way deeper into his heart every time he saw her.

~~~***~~~

The Darcy siblings boarded the carriage to return to Netherfield later in the morning. Both would rather have
~~~

stayed at Longbourn, but as they were not joining the family as Bingley was, could not in good conscience remain all day the way he did.

"What did you think of Miss Elizabeth?" Darcy was eager to hear his sister's opinion.

"I like her very much! You were correct in your assessment: she is fascinating. So very proper in every behavior but at the same time playful." Georgiana sighed. "I wish I could be half as confident as she appears to be."

"Miss Elizabeth has the advantages of experience and maturity to aid her. With time, your confidence will grow, as well."

Georgiana bit her lip and looked at her hands. "I hope so."

Darcy tilted his head as he looked at her, his brow creasing. He leaned across the coach, resting his hand atop her clasped ones. "Do not allow what happened this past summer to weigh so heavily on you. We all make mistakes, and Wickham is a charmer. Grown men have fallen for his schemes. What chance did you, a young girl, have against him?" He dipped his head to look at her down-cast face. "Georgiana?"

With a sigh, the young lady looked up. "My head knows this, but some-thing – some voice – inside me con-tinues to berate me. Loudly and per-sistently."

Darcy squeezed her hands, then let go and leaned back. "You must tell that voice to sit down and be quiet."

He smiled. "Can you do that? Eventually, it will have to listen."

Georgiana rolled her eyes and shook her head. "I do not know about that, but I will try. Thank you." She smirked as her brother laughed. "I love you."

"I love you, as well." Darcy looked out the window as the coach slowed. "We are here. Come; let us face the delightful Miss Bingley and then retire to the library for a game of chess."

"That sounds lovely!" She giggled as her brother waggled his eye brows and exited the coach.

~~~***~~~

Three days later, Darcy and his sister arrived at Longbourn's church with Bingley and his family. For Darcy, the previous couple of days had been
~~~

filled with sport, time spent with Georgiana, and brief visits to the Bennet family home.

Georgiana and Elizabeth had taken to each other immediately, a situation that elated Darcy. His sister needed a friend with sense, and Elizabeth certainly had it. He eagerly awaited each meeting with the lovely lady, and dreaded leaving. He looked at his friend with a certain degree of envy. If only he could stay all day, as Bingley did. He reassured himself that, with time, he would be in the same position.

Darcy descended from the carriage and looked around. He moved away to give Hurst room to step out, then handed Georgiana down. He drew her arm through his and nodded to a smirking Hurst.

"I see what you did there." Hurst shook his head. "Leave her to me, will you?"

Darcy grinned. "You know it." Hearing the other gentleman's chuckle, he moved away, his smirk dropping as the mask he wore when in public descended over his features. He led his sister into the church and to the front, settling her into a pew ahead of Sir William Lucas and his family. Taking a seat on the end, he helped Georgiana down next to him. He inclined his head so as to hear better when she leaned into him and whispered.

"You have done to me what you did to Mr. Hurst." She raised a brow. "Have you not?"

Darcy blushed and looked briefly away. "I apologize. Would you like to switch seats with me?"

Narrowing her eyes at him for a moment, Georgiana shook her head. "No, all is well. She can hardly lecture me here, can she? You may stay where you are."

Darcy squeezed his sister's hand. "I am in your debt. Let me know how I may repay your generosity."

At just that moment, Miss Bingley took her place in the pew on the other side of Georgiana, which put an end to Darcy's conversation with her. He smirked when his sister rolled her eyes, then turned his head forward. His breath caught as he spied Bingley leading Jane into a pew, followed by Elizabeth and the rest of her sisters, with Mr. and Mrs. Bennet bringing up the rear.

She is lovely, Darcy thought, as his gaze became fixed on Elizabeth. The service began, and he followed along, but his eyes rarely strayed from her light and pleasing figure. Almost before he knew it, the rector was walking up the center aisle and everyone was rising. He blushed and quickly stood.

A few moments later, he and his sister had joined the crowd filing out of the church. Darcy hated situations such as these, with people jostling him and whispering behind their hands about him. He flushed, his expression stern, as he steadily worked his way around lingerers and toward the door, his sister's hand tucked into the crook of his elbow. To his relief, they soon reached the rector, who stood at the entrance, speaking to the parishioners as they left. A brief exchange with Mr. Pound and the Darcys were standing in front of the building, waiting for the rest of their party.

"Fitzwilliam?"

Darcy's attention snapped from the doorway where Elizabeth and her sisters had just appeared, to Georgiana, standing at his side. "Yes?"

"May I go greet the Miss Bennets?"

"Of course. Stay where I can see you, though."

"Thank you; I will." Georgiana smiled at him before she turned and hurried across the way to speak to Elizabeth and her sisters.

As Darcy watched the group of ladies, a young man stepped to his side, and Darcy looked at him warily.

"Mr. Darcy." The man bowed. "Forgive me for approaching so precipitously. We were introduced recently at Longbourn. I am John Lucas."

Darcy bowed. "I remember; you are the brother of Miss Elizabeth's friend."

"I am." The young gentleman hesitated. "My sister, Charlotte, is close with all the Bennet girls, but Miss Elizabeth is her special friend. I consider her as one of my sisters."

A crease appeared between Darcy's brows, as he silently listened to the other gentleman, but he said nothing.

Lucas took his silence as permission to continue. He cleared his throat.

"I have noticed that you pay her a great deal of attention. You are not the first gentleman to reside at Neth-erfield to do so."

Now Darcy's brows rose. "Oh?"

Lucas gave a firm nod. "Two years ago, a family moved into the estate. The eldest son seemed to be enam-ored of Miss Elizabeth. He essentially ignored all the other ladies of the area and spoke and danced only with her. For months, he attended assiduously to her. We all expected him to make her his offer." He looked away for a moment but soon brought his eyes back to meet Darcy's. "He left for town one day and never returned. His family soon followed; within a day, if I recall correctly."

Dread filled Darcy's heart as he wait-ed for Lucas' next words.

"Charlotte and I were visiting Long-bourn a few weeks later, to comfort Lizzy as much as we could. She had known he was to visit town, but was disturbed and confused by his par-ents' disappearance from the area." Lucas paused again, for just a heart-beat. "We were perusing the newspa-per, hoping to distract her by discuss-ing current events, when she caught sight of the society section. Her suitor had married. His wedding announce-ment was at the top of the page. Lizzy was devastated. It has taken a long time for her to recover from her dis-appointment. She has rejected every man who has attempted to get close to her since."

Darcy could not hold back a gasp as he listened. Poor Elizabeth! If I knew who that gentleman was, I would find him and exact revenge for her. His face set in firm lines. "I am sorry to hear this. I tell you now that I would never do such a thing. My honor would not allow it."

Lucas nodded slowly, staring implacably into Darcy's eyes. "I am glad to hear it. However, just in case the thought ever does cross your mind, you should know that I will defend Lizzy's honor, to the death. Should you do as her previous suitor did, I will hunt you down and beat you to within an inch of your life."

Darcy stiffened and glared at other man. He ground his teeth as he paused, determined to remain polite despite his affront. When he was certain he could speak calmly, he did. "I assure you, that will not be necessary." Bowing sharply, he turned on his heel and strode toward his sister.

<p style="text-align:center">~~~***~~~</p>

That afternoon, following a light luncheon of bread and cheese, the residents of Netherfield, minus Bingley, who was spending the day with his betrothed, separated to their own amusements. Darcy first saw his sister to her chambers, where she and her companion were to pass the time working on some secret project or other. Then, he crept as quietly as possible to the library, tiptoeing past the drawing room where Caroline was engaged writing letters to her friends. He rolled his eyes in wonder at her having any but did not halt his forward movement. Finally reaching his destination, he locked the door behind him. Recalling a second door at the back of the room, he hastened to it and locked it tight, as well. Finally assured of his privacy, he settled into a chair in front of the roaring fire and thought about John Lucas and his warning.

By this time, Darcy's anger at the other man's presumption had waned. He was still aggravated by it, but he had begun to appreciate that Elizabeth had such a protector. It was apparent from the behavior of the matron of the family and her youngest daughters that Mr. Bennet had not taken the time to check them. Darcy recalled Elizabeth's murmured words during their dance about Kitty and Lydia. She was concerned for their futures. She should not have to be, he thought. That should be the purview of their father.

"She was hurt," Darcy whispered to the room, "and by a supposed gentleman." The image of Georgiana, hurt written all over her face when she learned that George Wickham had abandoned her, floated through his mind. "Elizabeth has suffered in a similar fashion to my sister." He bit his lip as he thought over his every interaction with the woman he had fallen almost instantly in love with. In hindsight, he could see evidence that she was, indeed, protecting her heart. She had been friendly – lively, even – and unfailingly polite, but never truly welcoming. "How did I not see this before?" he asked himself.

He sighed as the clock struck the hour. A glance at the mantelpiece and he could see that it was time for him to go up and prepare to dine. He pulled himself out of the chair and toward the door. He paused with his hand on the latch. "Should I give her up? I do not wish to be a cause of discomfort for her." His heart squeezed in his chest at the thought. "I cannot, so I will have to figure something out." Unlocking the door, he pressed the latch and opened it, striding through and heading to his rooms.

Chapter 6

At the appropriate time, Darcy exited his rooms and walked down the hall to his sister's. Mrs. Annesley opened the door at his knock, stepping back and inviting him in.

"Are you ladies ready?" Darcy smiled.

"We are, I think." Georgiana looked at her companion. "As long as Mrs. Annesley is, I am."

"I am ready!" The companion lifted her arm, where her reticule dangled. "I have everything I need right here."

Georgiana's eyes crinkled as she smiled and turned to her brother. "Then, we are, indeed, ready. We have prepared ourselves for battle."

Darcy chuckled as he shook his head. He held an arm out to each lady. "Hopefully, you will not need your weapons this evening, but it is good to be prepared, I suppose." He escorted them out the door and down the stairs.

The drawing room was empty when they arrived.

"I wonder where Miss Bingley is." Georgiana dropped her brother's arm and began to wander about the room, taking in the decoration.

Darcy assisted Mrs. Annesley into a chair by the fire. He looked up at his sister's words. "I do not know," he replied. "She prefers to be fashionably late sometimes. She will probably come down right before the bell is rung." He approached his sister. "What do you think of the painting?"

Georgiana startled from her contemplation of a landscape done in oils that hung between two windows on the side of the room away from the fireplace. "It is very nice. It looks rather familiar. I suspect it is a scene from some local spot. Would you not agree?"

Darcy examined the painting for a long moment. "You know, I think you are correct." He cocked his head, searching his mind for where he had seen that particular location. "I believe it depicts the field where we went riding the other day, along the border with Longbourn."

"That is it exactly!" Georgiana clapped her hands. "You have a good eye, and an excellent memory."

Darcy chuckled. "Thank you."

Miss Bingley chose that moment to wander into the room, followed by the Hursts. The three bowed to the Darcys, who returned the gesture. Then, they all chose seats. Darcy escorted his sister to a settee near her companion. He sat beside his sibling. Mr. Hurst had taken up space on a chaise lounge that was part of the grouping before the fire, leaving his wife and sister to sit on the sofa nearby.

"I understand my brother is spending yet another evening dining with those ridiculous Bennets." Caroline settled in. "He could do so much better than Jane. Why, he could have married any of a dozen debutantes with more to their name than Jane Bennet has." She sniffed. "I do not see the attraction, and he is saddling us with inappropriate relations that we neither wished for nor asked for."

Louisa glanced nervously at Darcy. "I think Charles is very happy, Caroline. Miss Bennet may not bring much monetarily, but she is everything lovely. There is more to life than money."

Caroline stared at her sister. "Are you insane? More to life than money." She shook her head. "Do you hear yourself?"

Louisa glanced over at her husband, who seemed to be asleep on his chaise lounge. "There is," she declared with a stubborn set to her chin.

"One day, you will discover this. At least, I hope you will."

Darcy listened to Bingley's sisters bicker back and forth, but his mind was not on their words. Instead, he was thinking again of Elizabeth and the sort of marriage he would have if he let her go and married anyone else.

He looked at Miss Bingley, sitting there going on about how poorly at-tired the gentry of the neighborhood were, and how uncultured, and knew that his life would be filled with such things were he to marry an heiress of some sort. He decided then and there he would not marry anyone like that. He would wed Elizabeth or no one. I will not give her up, he thought. I will woo her and win her hand. I will do whatever it takes to make her mine.

~~~***~~~

Darcy spent the next two days devel-
oping a plan to pursue Elizabeth. He
and Georgiana, along with Miss
Bingley and the Hursts, spent part of
each day at Longbourn. Bingley insisted his family get to know the Bennets better, and as the Darcys were
their guests, it was only natural that
they were invited along.

For Darcy, his time with the family
was eagerly anticipated. His sister
was making new friends with the
Bennet daughters, which was mostly
a good thing. Georgiana preferred the
three eldest girls and therefore spent
most of her time with them. He was
thereby given the perfect opportunity
to stare at Elizabeth and try to get to
know her by observing her. He made
note of her likes and dislikes, what
~~~

she read, and how she passed her time. He solicited her opinions on current events, which he knew she kept up with from his discussion with John Lucas. He was the first to offer his hand when she made to rise from her seat, and always offered his arm when the party walked the gardens.

"What are you about, Mr. Darcy?" Elizabeth asked the question with a smirk gracing her lips on the day before Christmas, as they chaperoned Bingley and Jane.

Darcy's brows rose above widened eyes. "What do you mean?"

"I mean, sir, that you have been most attentive to my every whim these last two days. There must be a reason for it. No gentleman would pay that much mind to a female without a reason."

Darcy was silent for a few paces, uncertain what to say. He eventually stopped and turned to face her. "I hope to prove to you that I am an honorable man. I understand you have been hurt in the past. I have come to admire you and wish to demonstrate to you that not all gentlemen are alike. Some of us are worthy of your esteem."

It was Elizabeth's turn to be quiet. She stared up at him. "I see." She paused. "I do not know where you obtained that information, though I could probably guess." She looked away, then returned her gaze to his features. "I wish you well in your endeavor. I **was** hurt, and I do not intend to allow it to happen a second time."

Darcy nodded slowly. "I understand. You are much like my sister, you know.

She also experienced heartache, just this past summer. I can see much of her in you." He turned to face the path again, holding out his elbow once more. When she tucked her hand into the bend, he looked down into her up-turned face. "I am sorry for your broken heart, and for Georgiana's. You may trust me, Miss Elizabeth." His eyes searched her face, and he wished he could brush his fingertips down her cheek. "I will never hurt you as that so-called gentleman did."

Elizabeth blushed, looking at her shoes. She said nothing, and they continued to follow his friend and her sister around Longbourn's gardens.

~~~***~~~

The next day was Christmas Day, and the families celebrated it quietly.
~~~

They remained within their homes. The Christmas Eve church service had been held at Longbourn's church with the Netherfield party in full attendance. After such a late night out, following as it was a long day spent with the Bennets, everyone concerned slept in. Darcy and Georgiana had, since their father's death, begun to exchange gifts on Christmas morning as a way to ease the pain of his absence. This year was no exception, despite their location. In Georgiana's sitting room, Darcy presented her with some new music and a hat from her favorite shop. She gifted her brother a set of handkerchiefs she had embroidered, and a pair of driving gloves made of the finest calfskin. The afternoon was spent in quiet activities: reading, games of chess and whist with their hosts, and the playing of Christmas songs on the pianoforte. Dinner that night was an elaborate affair with several courses.

Georgiana whispered to Darcy later, as he led her out of the drawing room and up to their chambers. "Miss Bingley must have been trying to impress you. That was quite a meal for the number of people in attendance."

Darcy rolled his eyes. "No doubt she was, but she has failed. Her ability to plan an elaborate dinner does not negate her other attributes."

Georgiana giggled, then kissed his cheek when he left her at the door to her bedchamber.

Boxing Day brought with it the promise of a dinner at Lucas Lodge. Darcy was looking forward to it, because Elizabeth was attending, and he had extracted a promise from her to dance with him, if the event offered such entertainment. The day dragged on, but eventually, the time came to bathe and dress, and the next thing he knew, he was handing his sister into the carriage for the ride to Lucas Lodge.

Darcy could feel his palms sweating in his gloves as they neared their destination. He stared out the window, his mind playing out how the evening might go. He startled to hear his sister's voice.

"Brother?"

"I am sorry. I was woolgathering. What did you say?"

Georgiana smiled. "No worries. I said I was excited to attend this evening."

"I am glad. Remember, though, that you are not out. You may not dance."

Georgiana shook her head. "I know I cannot." She shrugged. "I do not think I wish to, anyway. I have no need of a husband, and that is the purpose of dancing, is it not? To help one find a husband?"

"Well, I suppose in a way it is." Darcy hesitated a moment, the reminder of her recent heartbreak, as well as Elizabeth's, uppermost in his mind. "It can also be a way of passing time and enjoying oneself. It does not have to be only for husband-hunting."

"What about wife-hunting?" Georgiana smirked. "Do you enjoy it, or is it the method you prefer for finding me a sister?"

"I confess to disliking the exercise in general, unless I am particularly acquainted with my partner. However, with the right person, dancing can be great fun." He leaned back and looked out the window again. "I hope to have found your future sister." Turning his gaze back to Georgiana, he continued. "Only time will tell."

Georgiana's eyes widened at his words. "Is it Miss Elizabeth? Is that who you have decided upon?" Her voice rose in excitement.

"Calm yourself, Sister. I **have** chosen Miss Elizabeth. However, she has experienced a hurt similar to yours and it will not be easy for me to convince her I am not the same sort of fellow her previous suitor was. So, do not pressure her. Keep it to yourself, do you understand?"

Georgiana clapped her hands. "I will not say a word, I promise! I am so happy at your choice! I will pray for your success. I adore Miss Elizabeth!"

Darcy smiled, his nervousness all but forgot. The carriage slowed and came to a stop. Excitement filled him. He stepped out when the door opened and handed Georgiana out. They waited for Caroline and the Hursts, since they were also exiting their equipage. The group approached the door together, with Darcy and Georgiana in the lead.

Soon, they had been admitted to the house.

"Mr. Darcy! Miss Darcy! How good of you to come." Sir William Lucas greeted the guests with a great deal of enthusiasm.

"Thank you for inviting us." Darcy bowed as Georgiana curtseyed. "It is an honor."

"The honor is all ours, I assure you. I hope you enjoy yourself tonight." Sir William rose up on his toes for a moment. "Lady Lucas has planned a wonderful evening for us all."

Darcy nodded and smiled, then moved on to greet the lady of the house. Finally free of his duty to his hosts, he led his sister into the drawing room, where the guests were gathering.

"Miss Darcy, you have come!" Maria Lucas approached and curtseyed. "I am so happy you have. I did not know if you would be permitted."

Georgiana returned the greeting. "I am not allowed to dance, if any is planned, but since I will be sixteen soon, my brother thought it would be good practice for me to attend. My companion chose to remain at Netherfield. She had some correspondence to reply to."

"We will keep you company in her stead." Maria waved toward the other side of the room. "Kitty, Lydia, and Mary are near the fire. Would you like to join us?"

Georgiana looked at her brother, and when he nodded his permission, eagerly agreed to accompany her new friend to visit with the others.

Darcy looked on proudly. She is growing up into a fine young woman, he thought. With one eye on his sister and confirmation that the Bennets had already arrived, Darcy continued around the room, searching for Elizabeth. It was not long before he found her, deep in conversation with Charlotte Lucas.

"Good evening, Miss Elizabeth, Miss Lucas." He bowed to them with a smile.

"Good evening, Mr. Darcy. I am pleased you could join us." Charlotte returned his smile. "My parents love to entertain; I hope you enjoy yourself tonight."

"I am certain I will." Darcy glanced at Elizabeth. "Meryton is a pleasant town with pleasant people. I am honored to have been invited to join you all." He winced as Mrs. Bennet screeched something nearby. He cleared his throat and looked down.

"Well," Elizabeth said, flushing at her mother's indiscretion, "at least it is never boring here."

Darcy wished he could hug her and make her blush for other reasons than embarrassment. He sighed to himself. "No, it is not." He lifted his lips in a brief smile.

Charlotte looked between her friend and Darcy. "Did I see Miss Darcy arrive with you?"

"She did." Darcy tilted his head toward the fireplace. "Your sister approached immediately and invited her to join the group at the fire. Georgiana was delighted to be included."

Elizabeth turned and examined the girls. "Mary is with them. She will not allow your sister to be pulled into any nonsense my youngest sisters get up to." She turned back to Darcy. "I think, however, that Kitty and Lydia have been impressed with Miss Darcy's poise and have determined to behave more circumspectly this evening."

Darcy's brows rose. "Really?" He glanced at the group of girls. "I am happy to hear that."

"Yes," Elizabeth drawled, "I am, as well. I hope their resolve is strong enough to follow through."

Charlotte laughed, with Darcy joining in.

"Time will tell." He smiled at Elizabeth. "You have not forgotten your promise?"

"What promise is this, Eliza?" Charlotte nudged her friend.

Elizabeth blushed again. "I have promised Mr. Darcy that, if there is dancing this evening, he may have a set."

"Do tell." Charlotte glanced between them. "You did make a fine-looking couple at the assembly recently."

It was Darcy's turn to blush. "Thank you." He did not know what else to say, so said nothing.

Sir William's voice rang out over the assembled guests. "Dinner is served. Let us not stand on propriety tonight. Just come on across to the dining room and choose a seat."

Voices rose once more as gentlemen offered their arms to the ladies. Darcy held out his elbows to Elizabeth and Charlotte. He escorted them to the dining room and seated them in such a way that Elizabeth was between himself and her friend. During the meal, he was quite agreeably engaged in conversation with the woman he loved, as well as another neighbor, who sat on his other side. With Georgiana and her new friends across the table where he could keep an eye on them, he was quite pleased.

After the meal, the ladies separated from the gentlemen, moving back across the hall to the drawing room. Darcy was impatient with the tradition, but kept himself in check as much as possible when all he wanted was to be in Elizabeth's presence once more.

Eventually, Sir William rose and indicated the gentlemen should join the ladies. It was all Darcy could do not to run from the room. He forced himself to hang back and allow the others to walk ahead of him. However, when he followed them into the other chamber, his eyes immediately sought out Elizabeth, searching the groups of seated women until they fell upon her, standing with Jane, Bingley, and Charlotte near a window. He happily joined them.

"How are you enjoying the evening, Mr. Darcy?" Elizabeth arched her brow as she asked her question.

"I like it very well. The conversation at dinner was quite stimulating and the company exquisite." He smiled to himself as she blushed.

Charlotte tipped her head toward the corner of the room, where Georgiana and Mary were seated at the piano-forte going through the music. "It looks as though we may find our-selves dancing at some point, after all." She looked at Elizabeth. "You know what happened at the last dinner party."

"Yes," Elizabeth replied dryly. "My youngest sisters insisted Mary play music to dance to, and your father backed them up."

Charlotte chuckled. "That, he did."

Charlotte's prediction came true. Georgiana and Mary played a long concerto as a duet and when they finished, Lydia demanded music for dancing. Within a few minutes, the gentlemen had cleared a space in the middle of the floor and couples were lining up. Darcy was quick to claim his promised set.

"It seems the time has come, Miss Elizabeth, that you must fulfill your promise." Darcy bowed to her and extended his hand.

Elizabeth smirked and shook her head, but placed her hand in his. "So it seems."

Darcy greatly enjoyed his dances with her. He tried very hard to shed his natural reticence for the evening and get to really know his partner, and allow her to know him better.

Chapter 7

The next day, Darcy and Bingley rode into Meryton. They were unsurprised to find the Bennet girls standing in front of their uncle's law office, speaking to a group of redcoats.

Darcy nodded toward the gathering as he and Bingley rode toward them. "Rumors of a regiment wintering here were true, I see."

"Yes." Bingley nodded. "Feelings were mixed on it amongst the gentlemen I spoke to."

"It will be good for businesses." Darcy pulled his stallion to a stop.

"It will. However, many a young lady has had her head turned by an officer." Bingley dismounted.

Darcy mimicked his friend. "We must make certain that does not happen, then." He smirked, making Bingley laugh.

"Indeed."

The pair approached the group, leading their horses.

"Good afternoon." Bingley bowed. "How delightful to find you here."

Jane covered a laugh with her hand. "I told you we would probably walk here today."

Bingley grinned and winked. "So you did, my love."

Darcy watched his friend and Jane with a slight lift of his lips. He turned to Elizabeth, who stood beside him. "How are you this day? Thank you again for dancing with me last evening."

Elizabeth blushed but smiled. "I am happy you enjoyed it."

Darcy lifted a brow. "The question is, did you?" His attention was drawn to something behind her. A figure moved quickly away, ducking behind the shoppers milling about on the sidewalk across the street. His brow creased. He was certain he knew that gentleman. He felt an impulse to follow the other man, but Elizabeth's voice drew him back to his conversation.

"I did. Thank you, for asking now and for requesting a set in the first place."

Darcy grinned then. His next words were never spoken, because at that moment, over the noises of horses, carts, wagons, and people, came a scream.

"Fire!"

Darcy and Bingley both jumped at the word. They looked around, seeing citizens rushing toward the far end of the street, some with buckets. Darcy grabbed his friend's arm and turned to address the ladies.

"Go home and call your father."

Elizabeth shook her head. She began to strip off her pelisse, turning away from the gentlemen to address her sister. "Mary, take Miss Darcy and our sisters and go to Longbourn. Tell Papa there is a fire at the blacksmith shop." Elizabeth tossed the garment at her sister. "Jane and I will help with the water." She grabbed Jane's coat, as well, when it was thrust past her, and shoved it into another sister's hands. "Go! Now!" She shoved all four girls in the direction of Longbourn and turned to run toward the line of people, following Darcy and Bingley, who had abandoned the ladies and raced to help put out the fire.

The eldest Bennets joined the line that was forming near one of the water troughs that edged the main street of the town and began passing buckets back and forth. Full ones were handed off in the direction of the fire and empties were passed back to the trough to be refilled.

As the gentlemen approached the burning structure, they could hear screams from inside the building that was attached to the blacksmith shop. Knowing someone was within and seeing the fire licking at the wall that separated the two, Darcy plunged inside. He coughed when smoke filled his lungs.

"Is someone here? Continue calling so I can find you!" Darcy frantically searched the lower floor of the building, listening for the voice. Coming to a stairwell, he raced up.

At the top, he found a woman and two small children. "Come, we must get you out of here." Darcy lifted the babies, both old enough to walk unaided but still in gowns. "Follow me." He waited until the woman nodded, then turned for the stairs. He started down, the lady right behind him. He came to a sudden halt at the bottom of the steps, causing the children's mother to run into him. The path he had taken into the building was now being encroached upon by flames. Thinking quickly, he moved one of the children so that both were resting on one arm. He pushed their heads down into his shoulder, then reached around and grasped the woman's wrist. "We must run through it. Do not stop. Keep going. Do you understand me?" Seeing the woman nod, he tightened his grip, then faced the doorway, tucked his head into the shoulder of the child nearest his face, and began to move. When the woman stumbled, he did not stop, dragging her along behind him. After what felt like hours but was only seconds, they were through the flames and hands reached for them, removing the children and the woman from his grasp. He dropped to his knees and felt hands patting at his suit, followed quickly by water. He gasped.

"Darcy! Are you well?" Bingley's voice drew his attention, and Darcy looked up.

"I am." He coughed.

"Come." Bingley helped his friend to rise. "We need to get you out your of your coat. It is ruined. Caught fire." He peeled the garment off Darcy's shoulders. "It looks as though only your coat was touched. Let me look at your breeches."

Darcy stood still as his friend walked around him. He was still coughing up smoke now and again.

"You are one blessed man, Darcy." Bingley shook his head. "I see some singe marks but your legs did not catch fire."

"Good." Darcy coughed once more. "The children?"

"They and their mother have been taken across the street, I believe. Other than breathing in the smoke as you did, they all appear unharmed."

Bingley pulled Darcy further away from the men fighting the fire.

"The fire is not yet out. We should be helping instead of standing here." Darcy looked around. He spotted Elizabeth and Jane passing buckets. "There. Let us help over there."

Bingley followed his friend's finger and nodded. "Yes!"

The two hurried over to the line and took places beside their ladies. Darcy was upset to see Elizabeth exerting herself in such a fashion but did not have the breath to spare to express himself. Instead, he watched over her as they both worked.

Once the fire was out, Bingley and Darcy rounded up a wagon and horses to take the ladies home. After handing the Bennet ladies into the back, the gentlemen climbed up and sat on the front seat.

"Mr. Darcy!" Elizabeth's voice caught his attention. "What happened to your coat? Should we not go back for it?"

Darcy looked down at himself but immediately looked over his shoulder at her. His voice strained from the smoke he inhaled earlier in the day, he started to explain. "It is ruined. It caught fire."

As Elizabeth and Jane exclaimed in horror, Bingley stepped in to tell the tale. At the end, both ladies had their hands covering their mouths and their eyes filled with tears. Darcy, glancing back again, thought he detected a hint of respect in Elizabeth's gaze.

"You are … that was … I have no words. I know of no other gentleman who would risk his own life to save a stranger." Elizabeth paused. "My father would not."

Jane agreed. "Not rushing into a burning building. My father's abilities lie more in the area of supervising others."

Elizabeth explained further. "He is not unfeeling, he just ..." She trailed off.

Bingley turned in his seat. "All is well. Do not worry that we think less of Mr. Bennet for not being the sort to jump into danger. We do not. I did not do it, either. I will say, though, that I think if Mr. Bennet had been the first on the scene, he might have done just what my friend did." He glanced at his friend. "Darcy's legs are longer than mine or it might have been me who was the hero today."

Darcy shook his head, fighting to keep a smile off his face as the ladies giggled. He slowed the cart as he steered it off the road and into a driveway. "We have arrived at Longbourn."

As soon as the equipage stopped, Darcy descended, handing down the ladies. A rider cantered up the drive, stopping behind them. Darcy turned and looked at the gentleman as Bingley jumped down from his seat. "Mr. Bennet!"

Longbourn's master dismounted, wearily handing his reins to the groom who raced up to him. He nodded to the boy and trudged to where the young people stood. "Thank you for seeing my girls home."

"Are you well, Papa?" Jane took his grimy hand.

"I am well, my dear. Only tired." Bennet gestured to the house. "Please, gentlemen, do come in and have something to eat before you return to Netherfield. It is the least we can do for you; you did not have to risk your lives for the citizens of our humble village, after all."

Darcy exchanged glances with Bingley, nodding his approval.

"We would be happy to." Bingley's reply to Bennet came with a quick shrug of his shoulders. "I could not have walked away from the situation. I will be part of this family soon. What affects you, affects me."

The ghost of a smile lifted Bennet's lips. "Too true." He turned and stepped toward the door. "Come along, then."

Darcy and Bingley followed, each with a lady on their arm. Mrs. Bennet fluttered about, making sure all the gentlemen had something to eat and a cup of tea. Though it was difficult for Darcy, he bore with the lady's boisterous declarations of what might have happened to them, rushing toward a fire as they had. He was happy to witness the master take control of his wife, after he let her run on for a time.

Darcy and his friend did not remain above a half-hour. They were tired and sore, and stank of smoke. They took their leave of the ladies and Mr. Bennet and gratefully climbed into the borrowed wagon and headed back to Netherfield.

~~~***~~~

The following morning, Darcy escorted Georgiana and Mrs. Annesley into the breakfast room.

"Good morning!" Bingley stepped away from the sideboard and bowed. "I hope you slept well, Darcy."

"I did. I was exhausted." Darcy pulled chairs out for his sister and her companion, then moved to prepare plates for them. "Once my bath was completed, I fell into bed and never moved again."

Bingley chuckled. "I did the same." He picked up his plate of eggs, bacon, and rolls and moved to the table. "And you, Miss Darcy? How did you and Mrs. Annesley sleep?"
~~~

"Very well, thank you. The beds here are very comfortable." Georgiana looked at her companion. "Do you not agree?"

"I do." Mrs. Annesley smiled. "The pillows are exceptional, as well. I cannot imagine anyone not enjoying the rest they get here at Netherfield."

Bingley blushed with the praise. "Thank you. I will pass that on to my sister. We take great pride in providing the best for our guests, you know." He grinned, making the ladies laugh.

Darcy brought three plates to the table, each loaded with food. He set one in front of Georgiana, one in front of Mrs. Annesley, and set one on the table at his chosen place, on the other side of his sister. He seated himself and nodded when the footman brought the coffee pot to him.

"I plan to offer assistance to the blacksmith today. At the least, I can donate materials. Would you like to accompany me, Bingley?"

Bingley swallowed his mouthful of food, sipped his cup of coffee, and nodded. "I would. I plan to help, as well. Perhaps I can provide material for clothing. I can send an express to a contact in town and have him bring out several bolts of cotton from my mills."

Darcy nodded. "I am certain that would be appreciated." He looked at his sister. "Do you wish to ride along?"

"Oh." Georgiana glanced at her companion. "I believe Mrs. Annesley has something she needs me to do this morning. We had not planned to leave the house until this afternoon, when we are to visit Longbourn."

Darcy nodded. "Very well, then." He looked down the table toward his friend. "Are we waiting to see if your sisters and Hurst wish to come?"

Bingley's eyes widened. "No. As a matter of fact, if you are finished, why do we not leave now, before they come down?"

Darcy laughed. "Let me finish this last sip of coffee and I will be ready to go." Following his words with action, he stood as he set the empty cup on the table. He leaned down to kiss his sister's cheek. "I will see you later." With a nod to Mrs. Annesley, he followed Bingley out the door.

Chapter 8

Hours later, the entire Netherfield party climbed into Darcy's travelling coach for the trip to Longbourn. Conversation was minimal. Caroline would rather not be visiting the Bennets and seemed to have nothing to say now that she had been forced to attend them. Darcy and Bingley were holding on to their tongues by a thread because of Caroline's increasingly negative sentiments, which she did not fail to announce loudly and shrilly. Hurst and Louisa were trying to ignore the entire situation, and Georgiana and Mrs. Annesley were attempting to melt into the squabs.

After a tense ride, the group finally pulled up to Longbourn's door. Darcy descended first, followed by the rest of the gentlemen. Each assisted a lady down, and they approached the house. The door opened immediately upon their knock and within minutes, they were greeting the Bennet ladies in the drawing room.

As usual, Darcy's gaze immediately swept the occupants, looking for Elizabeth. He was happy to find her seated hear the fire on a settee. Once greetings were completed, he strode across the room to take the seat beside her.

"Good afternoon, sir. Have you recovered from yesterday's adventure?" Elizabeth smiled as she asked her question.

Darcy lifted his shoulders in a shrug. "I remain a bit fatigued and sore, but my throat is not as scratchy as it was when we last spoke." He looked her up and down. "How do you feel today? I am used to such exertions; after all, I regularly fence, box, and ride. You, however, are not."

It was Elizabeth's turn to shrug. "I am also sore. I have chosen to forgo needlework today because of it. However, I am in the habit of walking a great deal, so my pain and stiffness are limited to my shoulders." She nodded to the other side of the room, where Jane sat with Bingley. "Jane is the one who suffers today, though she will not speak of it."

"I am glad you are both well enough for visitors." Darcy paused. "If I may … I do not wish to be presumptuous, but I have had similar injuries in the past. It is better if you do not sit all day. Give the sore bits some exercise. A walk around the gardens might be helpful, even."

Bingley and Jane approached, having decided to sit nearer to Elizabeth and Darcy. They took seats on a chaise lounge on the other side of the seating area. Caroline followed, choosing a chair nearer to the settee where Darcy and Elizabeth were.

"I hope you are well, Miss Elizabeth, after our adventure yesterday?" Bingley smiled. "Jane tells me she is well, but I saw her wince when she lifted her arm just now." He turned his grin toward his betrothed, who blushed and looked down, making him chuckle.

Elizabeth covered her laugh with her hand. "I am well. I am more accustomed to exercise than Jane. However, we were both exhausted last night. I daresay you could have shot a bird in my room, beside my bed, and I would not have awakened."

"Is that so?" Bingley chuckled. "I was the same. It was difficult work but re-warding, because we were doing a service to another." He nodded to Darcy. "My friend here was at it again this morning. Neither of us could rest until we were certain the blacksmith and his family were taken care of."

Caroline had been silent all this time, but suddenly chose to speak. "What do you mean?"

Bingley's brows rose a bit. "Darcy has donated materials to rebuild the shop and its attached home, and I have made certain the family has cotton cloth for gowns and shirts and the like." He glanced at Darcy and then looked at his sister again. "I sent an express to town, requesting Mr. Harden send a wagon with enough cloth in it to clothe a family of four for a year."

"Well, I never …" Caroline's voice was sharp. "You would give away the source of our income? For a blacksmith's family? Whatever were you thinking?"

Bingley's jaw set, but his voice was mild. "We have a Christian duty to care for those who are not as blessed as we. I am merely doing my duty as a gentleman, Caroline. I recall many a time when Father did exactly as I have, to assist someone in need. Darcy has done the same."

Caroline sniffed. "Mr. Darcy can well afford such extravagance, though why he should do as you have is a mystery to me. The church exists to feed and clothe the lower classes. They should be left to themselves to work out their own lives. It was bad enough that you labored alongside them." She looked down her nose at Elizabeth and sneered. "You and the so-called ladies of this household."

Darcy had listened without speaking up to this point, though the blood had begun pounding in his ears. He heard Elizabeth gasp at the clear insult to herself and her sister and could bear to hear no more. "The church does not exist to maintain the lower classes. Its purpose is to guide all of us, of every class, along the proper path to salvation and, ultimately, our eternal reward.

"If you paid any attention to the services at all, you would know that we do, indeed, have a duty as Christians to assist those who cannot help themselves. That family's home and livelihood burned to the ground. They lost everything except the anvil and a few tools. They have nothing, no home, no furniture, nothing but the clothes on their backs, and no way of earning the funds they need. I did exactly as my father would have done and from what your brother is saying, what your own father would have done. Miss Bennet and Miss Elizabeth did the same. I suppose I should not be surprised at your opinion, though, with you being so closely tied to trade. At least your brother remains cognizant of his upbringing, even if you do not."

Caroline's face reddened deeper the longer Darcy spoke. In the end, there was nothing she could say. She stood and moved across the room to her sister's side, speaking only when spoken to and then in single syllables as often as she could.

Bingley cleared his throat. "Well. It is a bit chilly outside, but perhaps we could take a stroll in the gardens? Jane? Darcy? Miss Elizabeth?" He looked at each as he spoke.

Darcy nodded slowly. "Yes, it would be nice to get some fresh air." He turned to Elizabeth. "Will you accompany us?"

"I will." She stood. "I will let Mama know where we will be."

A couple minutes later, the four were promenading around the gardens.

Darcy offered Elizabeth his arm, which she took without hesitation.

"I apologize for losing my temper with Miss Bingley."

"I believe she may have deserved it. Do not trouble yourself with apologizing. You merely said what I wanted to but could not." Elizabeth glanced up at Darcy. "Thank you for defending me and Jane." She paused. "How long have you and Mr. Bingley been friends?"

Darcy shrugged. "I do not know … since Cambridge, at least. I think I was in my last year and he was just beginning his education when we met. That makes it something like eight or ten years."

She shook her head. "Is this the first time in all those years you have set Miss Bingley down?"

"Well, I did not meet her until his graduation, so I have only known her four or five years, but yes, this is the first time." Darcy sighed. "I have wanted to do it many times, and if she were not the sister of my very good friend, I would have long before now. It would be easier to walk away from her, but that would mean walking away from Bingley, as well, and that I cannot do. Finding friends as good, as loyal and faithful and honest, as he is a difficult task and I do not wish to lose that connection."

Elizabeth was silent for a moment. "I agree; finding good friends and keeping them is not easy." She smiled up at Darcy, and the look in her eye made his heart skip a beat.

~~~***~~~

"I have heard some delicious news, news that will separate Charles from that awful family forever!"

Darcy stopped just outside the sitting room door, where Caroline had made her announcement.

"Really?" Louisa sounded surprised. "I cannot imagine what that might be."

Darcy heard the rustle of silk, telling him Caroline had taken a seat. "The Bennet family is ruined." He clenched his teeth at the satisfaction in his hostess' voice.

"How so?"
~~~

"My maid just told me that Miss Lydia Bennet was found in a compromising position with an officer in the militia that was stationed nearby. It is all over Meryton, she said."

Darcy's brow creased. He felt guilty eavesdropping, but could not make himself stop. His heart started pounding as his thoughts darted to Elizabeth and what this meant for his pursuit of her. A name pulled him immediately back to the conversation.

"… Wickham. He is apparently from Mr. Darcy's home county. He refuses to marry the girl, as I understand it." Caroline paused. "We must inform Charles immediately, so that he may break off that farce of an engagement."

"I do not know, Caroline. He has already proposed and been accepted.

Even if he does not have a signed settlement, he has entered into a contract. I do not think he can break the engagement." Louisa's voice was tinged with doubt.

Darcy, needing more details and determined to help the Bennets, for Bingley's sake as well as his own, could listen no more. He strode into the room.

"Oh, Mr. Darcy!" Caroline's lips lifted into a smug smile. "Have you heard the news? Charles will be ending his engagement, as we will be moving back to town as soon as it can be arranged."

Reminding himself to remain calm and not let on he had heard her conversation already, he feigned surprise. "Oh?"

"Yes, of a certainty. You see, his future sister-in-law is ruined. She was seen behaving in a manner that no lady would, with an officer. Everyone knows about it." Caroline sniffed and lifted her chin. "No good family of breeding will have anything to do with any of them, not anymore."

Darcy ignored her commentary. "I have only met a couple of the officers, but none seemed dishonorable. Who was it that was caught with her?"

"A gentleman from Derbyshire, it seems; a Lieutenant Wickham. Are you, perhaps, acquainted with him?" Caroline's smirk remained in place.

Darcy gritted his teeth. "I am." He bowed. "If you will excuse me, I have some things I need to take care of." He turned on his heel and marched out of the room. Turning right, he hurried down the hall to the billiards room, where he knew Bingley awaited him. He finally came to a halt just inside the door.

"What-"

"Come with me. We have an emergency to deal with."

Bingley's eyes grew wide. "Emergency? What has happened?"

"I will tell you on the way. Come quickly." Darcy stuck his head into the hall and beckoned a footman. "Have our horses saddled immediately. There is no time to lose. We will walk to the stables to get them." He waved Bingley out the door, and the gentlemen strode to the entry hall and retrieved their hats and greatcoats.

"Clearly, whatever happened is serious. What is our destination? Do you have a plan?"

Darcy shook his head. "Not a clear one." He pulled on his outerwear and headed out into the cold December air. With Bingley on his heels, he marched down the drive to meet the horses, knowing they had moved faster than the message could have reached the stables. As he went, he explained the situation to his friend.

"Oh, my poor Jane! I will not give her up. I cannot. Even if my honor were not engaged, I love her too much to abandon her." Bingley's declaration was made through clenched teeth. "What of this officer? Can he be worked upon? What does Mr. Bennet say?"

"The officer is – was – my father's godson. He is a wastrel and the cause of much heartache in my family." Darcy paused in his explanation as they reached the stables, where the grooms were just finishing up with the saddles. He nodded his thanks to the boys, then swung himself up on Apollo's back. Seeing that Bingley had done the same, he nudged the horse into a walk. "I do not know Mr. Bennet's opinion. I just heard the story from your sister." He looked over at his friend. "I would not ask you to break off your engagement. You could not if you wanted to, not without being sued by Miss Bennet and her family. I did not say anything to Caroline about it, but I want you to know you have my support, no matter what happens here."

"Thank you. That means everything." Bingley paused. "I suppose my sister was gloating. How did she hear about it?"

"She was, and she apparently heard it from her maid."

"If that is the case, the news probably has spread all over the village." Bingley looked up and out over the countryside. "Are we to work upon this Mr. Wickham to get him to marry Miss Lydia?"

Darcy sighed. "That is probably the best choice. I did not know the scoundrel was in Meryton or I would have chased him away before." He shook his head. "Regardless, it will likely take a deal of money to per-suade him to marry her, though it may be that the threat of my cousin is enough to make him comply."

Bingley laughed. "The good colonel can be rather intimidating when he wishes. I hope it works."

Darcy chuckled, then fell silent.

Chapter 9

The pair rode to the militia encampment and asked to speak to the colonel of the regiment. Within moments, they were ushered into his tent, which was set up much like an office, with a table, chairs, and a Franklin stove that was emanating a great amount of heat, keeping the canvas structure remarkably warm. The officer stood when the gentlemen entered.

"Mr. Darcy. Mr. Bingley." Colonel Forster bowed. "Welcome." He gestured to the chairs in front of his desk. "Please be seated." When all three were sitting, he continued. "How may I be of assistance to you?"

Darcy cleared his throat. "I believe there is a man in your regiment by the name of Wickham?"

Forster tipped his head. "There is." His eyes darted from Darcy to Bingley and back. "What has he done?"

"He has publicly compromised a young lady of the neighborhood. I intend to see to it that he marries the girl." Darcy stared intently into the colonel's eyes.

"I see." Forster paused. "How can you be so certain it was not she who compromised him?"

Darcy's brows pulled together. "I have known George Wickham since my youth. He was my father's godson, and we grew up together. For many years, I cleaned up his messes, paying his debts and setting up situations for girls he had ruined, as well as the children he left them with."

"I see," the colonel said again. He sighed. "Mr. Wickham has not been with us long. I suspect I should be happy about that."

Darcy's lips twitched. "Probably."

"I will send for him." Forster rose. "Please wait here." He strode around the desk and stuck his head into a second tent attached to his. "Saunderson, please call Lieutenant Wickham to see me. It is urgent; whatever activity he is currently engaged in is to be halted at once and he is to report to me."

Darcy could not hear Saunderson's response, but Forster returned to his desk, offering hot coffee or tea.

"Thank you, no, not for me." Darcy gestured to Bingley. "My friend might wish for some, though."

"I am good. Thank you." Bingley began to ask Forster a series of questions.

Darcy watched his friend and the colonel interact. It never ceased to amaze him how Bingley could make himself so agreeable to everyone he met. Ten minutes passed in this manner before the tent opened to admit the man Darcy had hoped never to meet with again.

Wickham's eyes widened for a second when he saw Darcy standing in his commanding officer's tent. He quickly recovered, however, and a smirk spread across his lips. He bowed. "Darcy. How good of you to come see me here."

Darcy bowed shallowly. "Wickham. I believe you knew I would visit you, did you not?"

Wickham's smirk grew into a grin. "Indeed, I did. I know you well, old friend. I knew when I saw you across the street, paying such close attention to that girl, that you would seek me out sooner or later."

Darcy gritted his teeth as his anger grew. "You targeted Miss Lydia, then? What do you hope to get from me?"

Instantly, Wickham became serious. "Thirty thousand pounds."

Darcy heard Bingley gasp at his side, but ignored him. "What makes you think I would give you that much money for a girl who is not family?"

Wickham shrugged. "It is what you owe me for Georgiana. I knew when I saw you that day that you hope to become part of the Bennet family. Lydia was easy enough to charm." He paused. "You give me the money, and I keep my mouth shut about the incident. If you do not, I will spread her ruin all over Hertfordshire, then take the tale to London. You will be denied the woman you want and I will have my revenge."

Darcy shook his head, the blood pounding in his veins. "You did not love my sister. You loved her dowry."

Wickham shrugged. "I do not deny it."

Darcy took a long-legged step toward his nemesis. "You will marry Miss Lydia. I will find you a position in another regiment and fund one advancement, and I will give her one thousand pounds on top of her dowry."

Wickham laughed. "No, I will not marry her. I told you what I want."

"I do not care what you want." Darcy's roar shocked everyone in the room into muteness. "You will marry her. My cousin is on his way to Meryton as we speak. Surely, you will not deny him."

Wickham had grown pale at Darcy's words. He swallowed. "Very well, then. I will marry her. Fitzwilliam does not need to concern himself with it."

Darcy wanted to laugh at Wickham's obvious fear, but did not. Instead, he maintained the scowling visage that had gotten him this far. He turned to Forster, who had listened with rapt attention to everything that had transpired. "I prefer Mr. Wickham be sent back to his lodgings with a guard and not allowed to leave until the day of his wedding."

Forster nodded rapidly. "That can be arranged." He stood from behind his desk and hastened to Saunderson's.

Darcy watched the regimental commander go, then turned his gaze back to Wickham. "My father would be proud of you for doing the correct thing and behaving as a gentleman."

Wickham did not reply at first. He stared at Darcy, opening his mouth to say something but stopping when Forster returned.

"It is all arranged." The colonel gestured toward Wickham. "A guard will be here momentarily to escort the lieutenant to his quarters and will remain stationed outside his door until further notice." He turned to Wickham. "You are hereby suspended with pay for a fortnight or until I reinstate or dismiss you. You will remain in your quarters, and meals will be brought to you. I am ashamed that one of my officers would purposely damage a young lady's reputation as a means of revenge on another man. Your punishment will be reviewed in two weeks. You are dismissed."

Wickham narrowed his eyes at Forster but remained silent. Instead of speaking, he bowed at the colonel. He paused to sneer at Darcy and Bingley, then turned on his heel and walked out.

Darcy turned to Forster. "Thank you, Colonel. I appreciate your assistance in this matter, and that you are taking it seriously."

Forster bowed. "The lieutenant's actions were performed with malicious intent. I could not allow that to be brushed under the rug."

Darcy would have said more, but a shout arose outside the tent, accompanied by the sound of pounding hooves. Darcy, Bingley, and the colonel rushed outside to see Wickham riding away. Immediately, the two gentlemen mounted their horses and gave chase, followed close behind by a mounted guard.

The group did not have far to go to catch up with the fleeing man. They were no more than thirty yards behind him when his horse suddenly shied, stopped, and began to rear. Wickham held on, sawing at the reins to make the animal calm, but was thrown from its back. He landed on his neck, and the entire party behind him heard the crack. By the time Darcy reached him, Wickham was dead.

~~~***~~~

Immediately upon realizing his former friend's condition, Darcy began making plans. He and Bingley rode with the soldiers and Wickham's body back to the camp. He conferred with Forster, and requested the use of the colonel's desk and writing materials. Letters were sent to Pemberley and London, and a note to the local undertaker.

"What will you do with him? Bury him here?"

Darcy glanced up at Bingley before turning his attention back to his writing. "No," he said. "It would not honor his father or mine to do so. I will have
~~~

him sent home and buried with his parents."

"I will share the cost with you. I am certain Jane would wish me to do so." Bingley turned his hat in his hand as he stared at the other gentleman's swiftly moving pen.

Darcy shook his head, stopping his activity and looking his friend in the eye. "I will do it alone. I feel responsible; he was my father's godson, and Papa would have wished me to do this. He never knew the kind of man his favorite had grown into." He shrugged, feeling self-conscious. "It is the right thing to do," he added quietly.

Bingley nodded. "I understand. Even though Wickham was reprehensible, his father and yours were not, and you wish to honor them by treating him better than he deserves."

Darcy nodded. "Yes. That is it exactly."

"You are a good man, Darcy."

The side of Darcy's mouth lifted briefly. "Thank you."

~~~***~~~

It took a couple of days to get Wickham's body dealt with, encased in ice and charcoal in a coffin, and sent to Derbyshire. Bingley stayed by Darcy's side as they worked to deal with it, at the same time combatting rumors about the Bennets, which, they had discovered, had spread far and wide. Worried about their ladies, Bingley dashed off a note to Longbourn, handing it to the housekeeper with instructions for it to be sent off. Then,
~~~

he focused his attention on the events at hand.

"Thank you for that." Darcy was relieved to know Elizabeth would not think he had abandoned her. "I could not write, though I suppose a note to Mr. Bennet would not have been out of the question."

"No, but he may have used it to tease you with later. This way, the missive goes directly to Jane, who will inform the rest of her family."

Darcy nodded and grew quiet for a long while. Eventually, when he had completed the task of hiring men to convey the body north, he spoke again. "I cannot believe the neighbors have shunned the Bennets, and over such a small thing as a kiss."

Bingley shrugged. "You yourself have commented on the brashness of the youngest girls. I suppose they are not surprised that she would come to such an end." He paused. "I do not understand it, either, to be honest. She is what, fifteen?"

"The same age as my sister." Darcy paused. "Georgiana has been indisposed for a few days or she would have visited Longbourn without me." He took a deep breath. "Your sisters have refused?"

Bingley rolled his eyes. "They have, to my shame. I lectured them both quite harshly, though I do not know if it made a difference."

Darcy's lips pressed into a thin line. "Miss Bennet and her sisters are better off without Caroline lording it over them, anyway."

"True." Bingley shrugged. "I wish my sister were different. One can choose one's friends but not one's family."

"Yes, sadly. You are stuck with the family you are given, at least until you make a new one with someone else." Darcy glanced over at his friend, who had brightened with his words.

"Correct." Bingley laughed, sitting up straighter. "I will make a new family with Jane, and Caroline and Louisa can live their lives without us."

Darcy laughed with his friend and then turned his attention back to his task.

Chapter 10

A knock on the door of Bingley's study brought the gentlemen's attention away from their discussion.

"Enter." At Bingley's call, the housekeeper opened the door and stuck her head in.

"A Captain Carter is here to see you and Mr. Darcy, sir."

Darcy and Bingley looked at each other, brows raised. Bingley turned back to Mrs. Nichols.

"Send him in."

The gentlemen rose as the housekeeper opened the door wider and a young man in uniform entered and bowed to them.

After Darcy and Bingley had returned the captain's greeting, Bingley waved him into a chair. "What can we do for you, Captain?"

Carter cleared his throat. "I-, I-" He took a deep breath, turned red, and swallowed. "I heard what that Wickham fellow did to Miss Lydia." He paused and looked down. When he spoke again, it was so quietly done that Darcy and his friend had to strain to hear him. "I am … fond … of her." He looked up. "I would like to offer her my hand, if you think she and her father would accept me. I do not make as much as a senior officer, but I have an allowance from my father, and am to inherit a small estate upon my grandmother's death. I would take very good care of her. She will never want for anything." He stopped again, swallowing, and then, in an almost defiant tone of voice. "I love her. I was too shy to speak to her about it before, and I regret to my bones that I did not claim her the moment I knew my heart."

Silence reigned for a long moment. Darcy had not expected anything like this, and was certain Bingley had not, either. Finally, he found his voice. "I see." He paused, formulating his thoughts. "Why have you approached us instead of applying to Mr. Bennet? There is nothing Mr. Bingley and I can do, really."

Carter blushed and rubbed his palms on his breeches. "To be honest, sir, you and Mr. Bingley are closer in age to me than Mr. Bennet, which makes you more approachable, and it is possible he will not want a soldier to marry his daughter after what has happened." He shrugged. "I had hoped you might … pave the way for me with him."

Darcy nodded. "I can understand that. I suspect, and Bingley can tell me if he disagrees, but there is not a doubt in my mind that Mr. Bennet would accept you. I do not believe he is one to paint all people of a group with the same brush because one of them did something wrong. That being said, I do not know Miss Lydia's heart. What if she does not love you? Can you live with a wife you care for who does not return your feelings?"

Carter swallowed. "If that is the case, that she has no feelings for me, I will simply woo her and make her love me. I cannot live with myself if I walk away and she remains ruined, not when I can save her. She is a lady who needs society and respectability, and I can provide those to her, at least as far as she is already used to."

Darcy nodded slowly. "Very well. I commend you for your care. You will need to speak to Mr. Bennet, but I doubt he will turn you down, unless his daughter does." He stood. "Do you have time right now to ride over?"

The captain came to his feet. "I do. I requested the rest of the day off."

"Good." Darcy looked at his friend. "What say we take a ride over to Longbourn?"

"Yes, let us do that!" Bingley jumped up and strode to the door. Beckoning to the footman stationed just outside of the room, he ordered the horses saddled and brought around, then joined Darcy and Carter as they made their way to the entry hall.

~~~***~~~

The three were largely silent as they trotted the trio of miles to their desti-nation. Each was lost in thoughts of their own lady, and could spare none for the rest.

Darcy was taken aback at the surprise on the housekeeper's face when she opened the door to him and his com-panions. He ignored it, asking to see the master, then stepping into the hall as she scurried to Bennet's book room.

Seconds later, Mrs. Hill was back, taking the hats and coats of all three visitors and bidding them to follow her. Darcy's brow creased as he took in the deathly stillness of the house. It was highly unusual; the Bennets were
~~~

a lively bunch and he thought he at least ought to hear complaining about the lack of visitors. When they arrived at the book room, he smoothed his brow. He would find out later what was happening. For now, he must help resolve Miss Lydia's situation.

When the group entered following the housekeeper's announcement of their names, Bennet was rising to his feet. He bowed to them, and they each returned it. Longbourn's master was the first to speak.

"I confess I am surprised to see you all. My daughters were certain you had abandoned them, and when I did not hear from you, either, I was inclined to agree."

Darcy looked at Bingley, a crease forming again between his eyes.

Bingley looked back, a similar line on his face. "What do you mean?" Darcy turned his attention back to Bennet. "Bingley wrote Jane a note two days ago."

Bingley nodded vigorously. "Indeed. Did she not receive it?"

Bennet shook his head. "I was not informed of any letters. What did the missive say?"

"That Darcy and I were dealing with Mr. Wickham but would be by just as soon as we could." Bingley flushed from his cravat to his hairline. "I gave it to Mrs. Nichols, rather than my sister, and asked her to send it. I knew I could trust her with it. Something must have happened there. I will discover the truth of the matter as soon as I return to Netherfield, I assure you."

Bennet sighed. "I believe you must be telling the truth. I have to. You have given me no reason before now to think you a liar." He waved at the chairs in front of his desk. "Please have a seat. One of you will need to drag one from the table if you are all to fit."

Carter did as instructed, and brought a chair to sit beside the one Darcy took. Bingley was on the other side of his friend.

Seeing that they all were all seated, Darcy cleared his throat. "First, you are aware that Mr. Wickham was thrown from his horse and is now deceased?"

"No, I was not informed of it." Bennet blew out a breath and sat back. "I cannot say I am sorry to hear it."

Darcy shook his head. "Neither can I, to be honest." He gestured to the man at his right. "Captain Carter has expressed his admiration for Miss Lydia and his concern at her situation." He cocked his head. "I assume the neighbors have shunned your family? Rumors have abounded and Bingley and I have done our best to combat them, but we are strangers, essentially, and not family. I am uncertain our efforts bore fruit."

"You are correct, to my wife and daughters' utter distress." Bennet paused and turned to Carter. "You say this young man has expressed interest in helping Lydia?"

Carter stammered a response. "Y-, yes, sir."

"Why? I am certain you can understand my hesitation to simply accept the word of a soldier after what happened to her."

"Yes, sir, I surely understand that." Carter straightened and took a deep breath. "I promise you, I am nothing like Lieutenant Wickham was. You can ask my superior officers if you require a character. As I told Mr. Darcy, my officer's pay is not much, but my father gives me a stipend and I am the heir to a small estate in Sussex. I will be able to provide Miss Lydia with all the material advantages she enjoys in your home." He paused, swallowed, and blushed. "Additionally, I will provide her with all the emotional advantages she will allow. I-, I-" He started to stammer once more but stopped himself, swallowed, and began again, more slowly. "Over the course of our acquaintance, I have fallen in love with Miss Lydia." He looked her father in the eye. "I know she may not return my feelings, but I would like to marry her, regardless. I can persuade her to love me, and would prefer to court her properly, but I feel that it would serve her and her entire family better if we married right away. I can court her as my wife once we are wed."

Bennet nodded. "You have put much thought into this," He paused, his hands steepled in front of him, his elbows on the arms of his chair. He sighed. "I can see no impediment. If you were inclined to follow the path of Mr. Wickham, you would not have sought me out. If my daughter will have you, I give my consent." He rose. "I will call for her."

Darcy and Bingley rose, as well. "We should leave you to handle this privately."

Bennet nodded, but said nothing, his attention drawn by the housekeeper. After giving Mrs. Hill her instructions, he turned back to the gentlemen. "As you heard, I have had Jane and Elizabeth called down, as well." He gave Bingley a pointed look. "If I were you, I would be prepared to grovel. A woman who believes she has been spurned will be in no mood for shallow excuses."

Both men swallowed. Bingley's reply of, "No, sir, she will not," was drowned out by Lydia's arrival. They bowed to her, murmuring greetings, then silently exited the room, shutting the door behind them.

"The ladies await you in the front sitting room, sirs." Mrs. Hill curtseyed and glided down the hall to said room to announce them.

Darcy stepped into the chamber with Bingley following. They bowed, and he examined the countenances of each of the ladies as they rose from their curtseys. The three eldest daughters were in attendance, and all had red-rimmed eyes. They were pale, but each chin rose. Jane's eyes cast down, as did Mary's, but Elizabeth looked between the gentlemen before looking directly into Darcy's.

"Well, sirs," she began, a strong note of defiance in her tone. "I am surprised to see you here."

Bingley's voice was hesitant. "I promise you that I sent a letter with an explanation. Your father insists it did not arrive."

Darcy watched Jane look up as his friend spoke. She bit her lip. Her head shook. "We never got it."

"Perhaps we should ask Mrs. Hill to look into it, Jane. It is possible it was overlooked. Mama has been …" Mary trailed off as she glanced at the gentlemen. "She has been difficult. With the house in an uproar, it is entirely possible for a note from a neighbor to be laid aside to be dealt with at a later time and then be forgotten."

Everyone in the room took in a breath.

Jane pulled her eyes from Bingley to look at her sister. "That is an excellent idea." She hesitated. "Will you do it now?"

It was Mary's turn to pause, but at some unspoken communication from both of her sisters, she nodded and turned toward the door. The rest of the room's occupants watched her leave. Jane turned back to her betrothed, who took two steps toward her. Nothing was said; instead, the couple stared at each other.

Darcy looked from his friend to Elizabeth, who had also been watching Bingley and Jane. Darcy again noted the distress in her features, this time also seeing the clench of her jaw and the expression of anger and defiance in her eyes. Jane spoke, and they both startled at her words.

"We should sit. Mama is …" Jane paused. "Indisposed, and Kitty is sitting with her. They wished to visit with you but my mother needs her rest, and requires my sister's company."

The gentlemen perched on the edges of chairs near the settee where Jane and Elizabeth had seated themselves.

"Your family – Miss Lydia, especially – has suffered a serious blow. It is gracious of you to attend us at all when you are in such distress." Bingley spoke softly. "I am so sorry my letter did not reach you. I had hoped to avoid just such an occurrence by sending it."

At that moment, Mary rushed back into the room, an envelope in her hand and the housekeeper on her heels. "Jane! He did send a note!"

The Bennet ladies and the gentlemen had all risen upon hearing her voice. Mary paid no mind, instead running up to her sister and thrusting the missive into her hands.

Mrs. Hill drew everyone's attention when she unexpectedly cried out. "Oh, Miss Bennet, I apologize! When that letter was delivered, the house was in chaos, your mother needed her salts, and Miss Lydia was hysterical. I dropped the note in my apron pocket, thinking I would give it to you when I reached Mrs. Bennet's rooms, but then when I arrived, my attention was distracted and I completely forgot about it. I am so sorry!" She twisted her hands together as she spoke, then bit her lip as she awaited a response.

Jane, ever serene and clearly wishing to keep the peace, was quick to assure the housekeeper that she held no ill will toward her. "All is well, I promise you." She smiled. "These things happen, and Longbourn has certainly not been a calm, peaceful oasis lately."

Elizabeth snorted at her sister's words, but then covered her mouth and blushed. She cleared her throat. "I agree with Jane. You are not to blame for an oversight like this, not when your attention was pulled in several directions all at one time."

"Thank you." Mrs. Hill bobbed a curtsey. "If I may, I should apologize to the master, as well." When she was waved away, she hurried out of the room and toward the study.

Jane examined the outside of the envelope in her hand, touching her name.

"I know he is here now and could easily tell us what the note says, but I confess I would rather see with my own eyes. Hurry, Jane, and open it!" Elizabeth's attention had become focused on her sister and the letter.

Jane jumped a little, turning red and casting an annoyed glance at her sister, but obliged her by releasing the seal and unfolding the page. Her brows rose at the sight of the writing, which Darcy knew must be filled with blots, and she gave Bingley a wide-eyed glance before returning her gaze to the missive.

Elizabeth read silently over Jane's shoulder, her eyes growing large. She looked at Bingley, and then at Darcy, opened her mouth and then closed it, and then sat up straight, her eyes filling with tears and her chin trembling.

Mary huffed. "Are you not going to read it out loud?" Her cry startled everyone, and Jane immediately read out the contents for all to hear.

"Well," Mary said when her eldest sister had finished. "I did not believe for a minute that Mr. Bingley would abandon us so cavalierly, despite what Mama said." She nudged Elizabeth, beside whom she had seated herself when Jane began to read. "And you. You were positive we would never see anyone from Netherfield, ever again."

Elizabeth took a deep breath. "You are correct, I did." She turned to the gentlemen, but her gaze was focused on Darcy. "I owe you an apology. You are nothing like-" She stopped. "You are an honorable gentleman. You both are. I should never have doubted you. I am sorry. Ashamed and sorry."

"Oh, Charles, I am, too." Jane started to sob and instantly, Bingley was at her side, kneeling by her chair and pulling her into his arms.

Elizabeth could not hold Darcy's eyes. Her own tears began to fall. He immediately stood and approached, holding out his handkerchief to her. When she took it, he stood before her, wishing he could hold her as his friend was holding her sister.

Elizabeth wiped her eyes and, looking up at Darcy with an expression that made his heart pound, held it out to him. When he accepted it, she did not remove her fingers, and he curled his over them.

He pulled her to her feet. "Miss Elizabeth," Darcy whispered. "Have your opinions of gentlemen who live at Netherfield changed?"

"My opinion of one gentleman who resides at Netherfield has always been good. It was only that it was difficult to trust that what I saw was true."

Darcy stopped breathing momentarily. "And now?" His heart pounded as he waited for her reply.

"Now, I know that some gentlemen are worthy of my trust." She looked up at him, her eyes searching his, and lifted her lips in a small, barely-there smile.

Darcy swallowed hard. "In that case, will you join your life to mine and allow me to prove to you over and over again that I love you and will never leave you? Will you marry me?"

Elizabeth's eyes filled with tears once more and she nodded. "Yes," she whispered. "I will."

Joy filled Darcy's soul as he heard her consent. He lifted her hand to his lips, pressing a gentle kiss to her knuckles. "Thank you. You have made me the happiest of men." He leaned forward, eager to caress her mouth with his, when a movement at his side made him pause.

Mary was looking at him, one brow raised. "Congratulations, Mr. Darcy. Congratulations, Lizzy. Clearly, you are in need of a chaperone. I will be happy to take on the task."

"Oh, Mary." Elizabeth sighed. She looked longingly at Darcy's lips.

"Thank you for your offer." She looked up at her betrothed. "And thank you, too, for yours." She smiled, this time more brightly.

Darcy cleared his throat. He flushed, glanced at Mary, and then looked at his beloved. "Thank you for accepting me." He stared into her eyes for a bit longer before saying, "I should speak to your father."

Elizabeth nodded. "Is he done with Lydia?"

"I do not know. I would hate to interrupt him, but on the other hand …"

"He might appreciate the interference." Elizabeth smiled.

Darcy grinned back and turned, offering her his elbow. "Shall we do it now?"

Elizabeth laughed and tucked her hand in the bend. "We shall."

They were interrupted in their quest by Bingley and Jane, who offered their congratulations, but were soon knocking on the door to the study.

Netherfield Hall

Twelfth Night

On the evening of the second full day of their engagement, Darcy and Elizabeth stood together in the receiving line at Bingley's long-planned Twelfth Night ball. Though the news of the engagements of three of the Bennet daughters had quickly spread through Longbourn, Meryton, and the surrounding areas, the decision had been made to announce them all before the dancing began. Bingley and Jane, followed by the Hursts, then Caroline, were the first to greet the guests and accept congratulations. Next were Darcy and his betrothed, followed by Lydia and Captain Carter.

Darcy had noted early in the evening that every time Caroline looked at him and Elizabeth, her nose lifted higher in the air. Given that she looked like she had encountered a foul smell each time she did, he was grateful that she chose not to speak. He knew, however, that she had been told to temper her responses if she wished to be welcomed to Pemberley with the rest of her family.

True to his word, before the musicians started, Bingley climbed up on the platform and called for everyone's attention.

"Thank you all for attending this evening. It is a very special one, and not only because it is Twelfth Night. No, it is important because my friends and I have an announcement to make." He bowed when his guests began to clap. Then, he gestured to Darcy and Carter, who both joined him. "Now then, you see before you three of the happiest men in the kingdom. Many of you are aware that a few weeks ago, I asked Miss Jane Bennet to be my bride, and she accepted me." When cheers and applause broke out, he thanked them. "My friend Darcy, the tall gentleman standing beside me, for those who have not yet had the pleasure of being introduced, just two days ago made an identical request of Miss Elizabeth Bennet, and on the same day, Captain Carter proposed to Miss Lydia Bennet. Both ladies graciously accepted. We plan to marry at the end of the month. There are negotiations afoot to bring about a triple wedding, but a decision on that has not yet been made." Bingley gestured to the musicians, and he, Darcy, and Carter descended to the ballroom floor as they began to play.

The couples were inundated with congratulations, even in the middle of their dances. Darcy bore it with as much grace as he could muster. He was happy to be out from under Mary's watchful eye for once, though, and silently resented all the intrusions into his time with Elizabeth. He stuck to her side the entire night, except when he was required to give her up to someone else for a set. It was during one of these intervals that John Lucas approached him.

"Good evening." Lucas grinned and bounced on his toes, much the way his father was known to do.

Darcy eyed him for a long moment, then bowed his head in acknowledgment. "Good evening."

Lucas gestured toward the dance floor, where Elizabeth had partnered with Hurst. "I see you convinced Lizzy to accept you."

Darcy stiffened. "It seems I did."

Lucas chuckled. "Be at ease. My sister made it clear to me why her friend has done so. I congratulate you."

"Thank you." Darcy felt himself relax a little. "I love her very much. I have no intentions of hurting her."

Lucas nodded. "I can see that. I watched you charge into that burning shop recently and knew that if Lizzy heard of it, you would rise in her esteem. Not that I believe you did it for that reason. You just happened to be at the right place at the right time. But I know Lizzy, and that sort of leadership is attractive to her."

Darcy did not know what to say, so he nodded and let Lucas continue.

"Well, anyway, you have shown her that you respect her and that you are a gentleman who deserves the name." Lucas smiled. "Though, I still say, if you hurt her, I will make you regret it."

Darcy rolled his eyes and shook his head. "Very well. I have been warned." He stuck his hand out. "Thank you for your care of her."

"I could have done no less. I knew it would take someone like you to turn her head." Lucas smiled, tipped his head, and sauntered away.

The music soon ended, and Hurst returned Elizabeth to Darcy's side.

"What has you smiling so, sir?" Her brow arched in a way that left her betrothed wishing he could kiss her.

"Oh, nothing," he said as he lifted her hand and kissed her fingers, since he could not have her lips. "I was just thinking about the scheme I devised to win your hand, and how, in the end, it was something totally unrelated that made you love and trust me."

Elizabeth hugged his arm to her side. "Thank you for being so persistent. I would have been broken-hearted had you left without trying."

Darcy's brows rose to his hairline. "Really?"

Elizabeth winked. "Yes, really. I loved you well before I trusted you. Now tell me about this scheme."

Darcy laughed. "Oh, no. The battle is won. I never have to think about it again." He gazed adoringly into her eyes. "I love you."

"I love you." Elizabeth's whispered words filled his heart with joy and his imagination with a view of their life to come, together.

The End

Before you go …

If you enjoyed this book, please consider leaving a review at the store where you purchased it.

Also, consider joining my mailing list at

https://mailchi.mp/ee42ccbc6409/zoe burtonsignup

~Zoe

About the Author

Zoe Burton first fell in love with Jane Austen's books in 2010, after seeing the 2005 version of Pride and Prejudice on television. While making her purchases of Miss Austen's novels, she discovered Jane Austen Fan Fiction; soon after that she found websites full of JAFF. Her life has never been the same. She began writing her own stories when she ran out of new ones to read.

Zoe lives in a 100-plus-year-old house in the snow-belt of Ohio with her Boxer, Jasper. She is a former Special Education Teacher, and has a passion for romance in general, Pride and Prejudice in particular, and stock car racing.

Connect with Zoe Burton

Email:
zoe@zoeburton.com

Facebook:
https://www.facebook.com/ZoeB
urtonBooks
https://www.facebook.com/group
s/BurtonsBabes/

Pinterest:
https://www.pinterest.com/zoebu
rtonauthor/

Instagram:
https://www.instagram.com/zoeb
urtonauthor/

Website:
https://zoeburton.com

Join my mailing list:
https://mailchi.mp/ee42ccbc6409
/zoeburtonsignup

Support me at Patreon:
https://www.patreon.com/zoeburt
onauthor

Me at Austen Authors:
http://austenauthors.net/zoe-
burton/

More by Zoe Burton

Regency Single Titles:

I Promise To…

Lilacs & Lavender

Promises Kept

Bits of Ribbon and Lace

Decisions and Consequences

Mr. Darcy's Love

Darcy's Deal

The Essence of Love

Matches Made at Netherfield

Darcy's Perfect Present

Darcy's Surprise Betrothal

To Save Elizabeth

Darcy Overhears

Merry Christmas, Mr. Darcy!

Darcy's Secret Marriage

Darcy's Christmas Compromise

Darcy's Predicament

Darcy's Uneasy Betrothal

Darcy's Yuletide Wedding

Darcy's Unwanted Bride

Darcy's Favorite

Victorian Romance:

A MUCH Later Meeting

Westerns:

Darcy's Bodie Mine

Bundles:

Darcy's Adventures

Forced to Wed

Promises

Mr. Darcy Finds Love

(available exclusively to newsletter subscribers)

The Darcy Marriage Series Books 1-3

Mr. Darcy, My Hero

Coming Together

Christmas in Meryton

The Darcy Marriage Series:

Darcy's Wife Search

Lady Catherine Impedes

Caroline's Censure

Pride & Prejudice & Racecars

Darcy's Race to Love

Georgie's Redemption

Darcy's Caution